A TOXICVERSE DUET
PART ONE

ARSYN QUINN

Cover Design: getcovers
Editing: Toxic Love Publishing
Proofreading: Nicole at Naughty Nook PR
Formatting: Nicole at Naughty Nook PR

ISBN: 979-8-9994534-1-9

Author's Note

This book is cursed I swear. I lost one completed draft and nearly lost another. This was hell to put out. But Xavier insisted.

The memories in this work are presented out of chronological order. This was intentional as I wanted them to come up organically.

This is in no way a safe or accurate depiction of kink, this is set in a world where safe words exist, and the characters actively chose to ignore that fact. As such this should not be used as an instructional tool for kink in any matter. Much of what is depicted is not safe in any way. Please do your own research before experimenting with anything you may find in this book.

Triggers are not meant to be an exhaustive list, I may have missed some

WARNING Incoming Cliffy. And I'm not sorry.

To anyone who has ever felt like a second choice.

Content Warning

This book contains the following themes and topics. Please review them. Your mental health matters.

Imprisonment
Prison Escape
Murder
Human/Sex Trafficking
Child Trafficking
Kidnapping
Threat of violence against a child
Marijuana and Tabacco Use
Stalking
Mentions of child abuse
Mentions of suicide
Mentions of child pornography
Depression and Anxiety
Torture
Blood and Gore

Non-Con/Rape

Forced Marking

Mentions of previous captivity

Mentions of SA and rape

Mentions of physical assault

Mentions of drugging

Blood consumption

On-page medical trauma

Playlist

I Stand Alone-Godsmack

You Broke Me First-Our Last Night

I'm Not Pretty-Jessia

Never Say Never-Cole Swindell and Lainey Wilson

Not Like Us-Kendrick Lamar

Red Room-Brice Savage

I Hate Everything About You-Three Days Grace

Fire Up The Night-New Medicine

Burn It To The Ground-Nickelback

Bleed It Out-Linkin Park

Enough-Cardi B

Monsters-All Time Low and Demi Lovato

Die A Happy Man-Thomas Rhett

Shatter Me-Lizzy Hale and Lindsey Starling

Battlefield-SkyDaddy

Tourniquet-Evanescence

Break Stuff-Limp Bizkit

Slayer-Brice Savage

Harder To Breathe-Letdown

Distraction-Kehlani

What's Your Fantasy-Ludacris and Shawnna

Can I-Kehlani

What If I Don't-Shaylen

Chains-Nick Jonas

Broken-Seether and Amy Lee

Its Not Over-Daughtry

Resource Guide

Local to the US; your numbers may vary.

National Human Trafficking Line

888-373-7888

Text INFO to 233733

RAINN Sexual Abuse Hotline

1-800-656-4673

Suicide Hotline

988

Trevor Project

866-488-7386

Text START to 678-678

Prologue

Rhys

The buzzer overhead was an annoying reminder of where I had spent the last twenty years. It was a prison-wide system that marked the passing of the scheduled day. It would have marked the passing of *my* day if I wasn't confined to a section of the prison known as serial killer's row. Here we didn't get anything but the legally mandated one hour per week of rec time, if we were lucky, something we often weren't. There were long stretches where we didn't leave the four walls we were confined to.

All we had here was time.

That was the worst thing that men like me could have on their hands. I spent the time I had studying the plans to the prison I had managed to get . At the moment, I had the blueprints to my section laid out on the bed. The plan had to be flawless, there was no other way this would work. The guards worked on a schedule, just like everything else in here. They would come soon, and when they did, I had to be prepared. Today was the day I escaped, it had to be. I couldn't take one more moment in this room. I was going to leave here in a coffin anyway, what did they care about my sanity?

There was only one kink in my plan.

From my count, there was a second alpha and an omega here. Not that the guards had checked our designation before housing us. There was a myth that alphas didn't commit serial murders all that often. That simply isn't the truth. Alphas killed as often as betas did, with more viciousness; our kills were often mistaken as animal killings. There was a case that just hit the news not long ago, someone called the Blue Ridge Butcher. He had to be an alpha, no one but an alpha would be so ruthless. The truth was, we were just better at not getting caught than other designations. It took more to turn an alpha truly feral.

Well, most of us anyway.

The alpha that was in the cell next to me was obsessed with a Mexican-American author. He systematically picked apart three of her potential packs before he slipped and ended up here. I wasn't truly sure why the omega was here. Regardless, I was taking him with me when I got out of this place. Working out the steps of my escape plan was really the only thing I could do to keep from losing my mind. Like clockwork, the door to my cell opened; it was an older system that operated on keys. They hadn't updated this part of the prison yet, which was a stroke of luck for me. I was up and moving before the guard was all the way inside, the shiv in my hand finding its home in his neck. I reveled in the feeling of the blood covering my hand, knowing that as soon as I pulled it from him I would be ending his life. That was one of the major things that most people got wrong; it wasn't the insertion of whatever you might choose that did the actual killing. It was the removal that caused the ultimate demise. Unless you got unlucky and cut something vital. I was a hair's breadth away from the artery where I had chosen to sink the blade home, close enough that if I wiggled the shiv I would open it right up. I did just that, twisting the handle as I removed it.

I held the body upright, using it as a shield to get close to his partner. He saw me coming, throwing his hands up in a bid to protect himself. It didn't do him any good when I threw the body at him. He landed on the floor beneath the corpse with a thud. It was justice to see the terrified look in his eyes knowing that he saw his death staring back at him. I moved across the room, shoving the blade into the second guard's throat and removing it just as quickly. From the things I had heard them talk about doing to that poor omega, their deaths were too easy.

I needed to get moving and I needed to do it now.

Kneeling down, I stripped his body, taking the baton and taser. Moving on instinct, I went to the alpha's cell first. The look he gave me when I opened the door made me hesitate, he was volatile and dangerous. A wild card that I couldn't afford if I was going to get the omega out of here in one piece.

"I'm not a fucking liability," he growled at me. "But if you leave me here I damn sure will be."

"Fine, but we get the omega to safety."

There was something in his eyes when he spoke to me again that told me I could trust him.

Temporarily.

"No fucking shit."

That was all I needed to hear from him. I moved from memory, coming down the long hall until I was standing outside the omega's cell. He was housed as far away from me and the other alpha as they could get him. Maybe that was the warden's way of trying to protect him. In fact, it did the opposite, leaving him more vulnerable to the guards that loved to prey on the omegas in the prison; the guards like the two I had killed. They loved to brag about all the fucked-up things they did to the omegas they had access to. Most people thought that the prisoners were the worst things here. We all knew differently; the men and women that ran this place were the real threat, and each of them was on my future victim list as soon as I got out of here. I moved to the end of the hallway, rage gathering in my gut at the thought of how isolated he was.

Omegas were to be cherished, loved. They were never meant to be vulnerable. Rage filled me at the thought of him being in there alone. Most omegas ended up in the special ward with nests instead of cells. They were still treated like they were precious, even in here. His treatment was abhorrent. The other alpha crowded me as I reached up to open the omega's door. My elbow came up, catching him in his stomach. It was enough to make him give me the space I needed; I didn't want this omega to fight me when I took us from here. Pushing the key into the lock, I held my breath as I pulled the door open. The omega's scent slammed into me like a wall. Anxiety and fear laced with what should have been a pleasant scent, making it bitter. I barely managed to keep hold of the beastly side of me when I thought of what he'd been through. All that mattered was getting him out, getting him safe from the horrors this place had heaped on him. I moved as slowly as I could, letting him get a feel for my scent. As soon as it hit him he leaped at me, my arms reaching out to catch him. He was shaking as I held him there. He didn't know me, but from his reaction, he must have felt safe with me. The shaking was pissing me off even more and I didn't even have anyone to aim all of that rage at. My hand came up to clear his hair from his eyes, allowing me to see his amber gaze for the first time.

"Can you walk?" I was whispering as I moved, heading toward the doors to the rec yard.

He wiggled until I let him down, smiling at me as he moved back to stand by the other alpha. "I'm Liam."

"Rhys." I nodded as I pushed out into the rec yard.

The alarms were blaring as the other alpha answered Liam. "Landon."

They crowded around me as I moved toward the hole I had cut in the fence. "We go through the hole one at a time. Liam first, then me and Landon."

I was pulling the fence to the side when I heard the rush of guards running into the rec yard behind us. Liam was small enough that he was able to get through the opening easily. Running full speed, he disappeared by the time I managed to make it through the hole. Landon was right on my tail, pushing through the fence as we sprinted into the neighborhood surrounding the prison. Liam wasn't too far ahead of us by the time we cleared the surrounding streets. We were deep into the area when we stopped. Choosing a house at random,

Landon kicked in the door. Picking out clothes and hot-wiring the car took less time than I expected, allowing us to get on the road in no time.

Landon took off from there, thanking us for the help with his escape. I never expected to see him again. Liam stayed with me, huddled in the passenger seat. It wouldn't take me long to get where I was going, so that gave me plenty of time to get the omega stashed somewhere safely. I was going seventy toward the wild spaces between cities. I knew just the place to put him until I could get him home. Pulling off the highway, I cut through traffic until I was on a two-lane road. I took a quick left into the woods, before pulling up in front of an abandoned cabin. This was the perfect place to lay low and plan our next moves. What those would be, I wasn't sure yet. I did know that there was one person I needed to find. I didn't know her name, but I did know that she was mine. I'd known the moment I'd heard her laugh on that tape.

Chapter 1

Penelope

Waking up in the nest wasn't something I cared to do on a regular basis, at least not *this* nest. My hand tightened on the duvet that had long ago lost Dante's scent. That should have made being here all that much easier, but it was the opposite. It made me ache for him even more. Knowing I couldn't touch him made it so much worse. When I'd agreed to this I had no idea that I would essentially be kicking Dante out of his personal space. And that's exactly what had happened, no matter what my intentions may have been.

Impact over intent.

I repeated the mantra in my head that my best friend, Amani, had given me a few weeks ago. I had to remember that no matter how pure my intentions may have been, how it made the other person feel was all that mattered. And my being here was making life miserable for my sweet omega mate. Leaving had always been part of the plan; I couldn't stay here. As much as I knew I had to, I couldn't bring myself to begin—couldn't start to let go. I had spent the better part of a decade trying to do just that. And when I needed a place to go, Dante opened his home to me. Something that no other omega on the planet would have done. It was rapidly becoming time for me to plan my exit.

The longer I stayed, the clearer it became, and Dante certainly wasn't making any of this easier. Not that I deserved any better from him, I was an omega after all. An unbound one around his pack, his men. Yes, we grew up together, but I had abandoned all expectations when I left them. Dante could ask me to leave, and I would, without a fight. He deserved that much respect. But try as I might, I was starting to hope there might be a chance for us to make this work again. The other omega was all but avoiding me. When we did encounter each other, he was short, almost cruel at times. Every second I was in this house was agonizing. I was so close to the only man in the pack I craved but he was so far from me.

When I came here, I made Richie promise me I wouldn't be bothering Dante or the rest of the pack. I was starting to think he lied to me. If he hadn't, then I was definitely the reason the other omega hadn't been in the room since Richie brought me home. I should've regretted answering Richie's call, but coming to help those omegas when they needed me gave me a sense of purpose, one that I desperately needed. Finding myself again after being trafficked was the hardest thing I'd ever had to do. It was a fight every day to stay moving, stay awake. To fight that hopeless feeling that was always there, waiting to drag me back into those terrible memories. But Dante's twin, Calliope, an alleged former serial killer, knew exactly what to do. She gave me the push I needed; calling me in to comfort those omegas was a stroke of genius. I needed to swing by and check on them after work.

My phone rang before I made it completely out of bed. "I'm coming, I must have overslept."

"You aren't late, Penelope. I'm afraid I have some bad news." My boss was calm, but then we were trained to be.

"You aren't firing me, are you?"

"Nothing like that." She took a breath. "We received a call about an escape from the prison this morning."

"Since when does that warrant a personal call instead of just telling me during the daily briefing when I get in?"

"One of the escapees killed your mother." She blurted out.

Rhys Kelly was the worst thing that had ever happened to me, and it happened before I could even form memories. There's nothing quite like everything in your life being tied to a notorious serial killer. Over the years, I had been contacted for interviews, declining every request as they came; there were plenty of survivors for them to talk to. Besides, staying out of the spotlight was easy for me. It was even a benefit at times, considering what I was about to do with my spare time. "Thank you for letting me know. I'll be in soon."

I hung up before she could reply. There was only one thing I needed to do. Moving to my travel bag, I pulled out one of the burner phones Cain set up for me. My brother was a sweetheart, taking care of everything I needed. Especially when his parents adopted me after my mother was murdered. He was always there with me, looking out for me like an older brother is supposed to. We had very different childhoods; he was trained to kill, trained to take over the family business. As such, he was kept away from kids his own age. Homeschooled in things that most children never have to think of. Meanwhile, I was permitted to go to school, make friends, and find my pack. Cain was the gentle one of us, hating to kill; he had to be taught to not feel, how to turn off the emotions. Our parents created the perfect killing machine. He eventually followed in their footsteps, joining the CIA, and heading his own task force. Along the way, he had found love, something I was holding out hope to achieve for myself.

They had gotten it all wrong choosing Cain for that. I was the detached one. I had to force myself to feign human emotion; more likely to lash out with violence than I was to be nice to someone. Cain had a love and compassion that gave me hope for the world. I also found that in Dante, and eventually his pack. That's the crux of the issue. They were *his pack, his men*. I had no claim on them, I gave that up long ago. Tucking the phone into my pocket, I turned back to the bed. Leaning down, I pressed a kiss to Richie's cheek before sliding out the door. Bradley met me in the hallway with a cup of coffee and a kiss.

"Morning, little troublemaker." The way he said it made me blush.

"Good morning."

He passed me the coffee he made. "Dante is in a mood."

"When isn't he?"

"I know it's been difficult," he brought his hand up to rest on my cheek, "He will come around soon."

He placed his hand on my shoulder as I moved past him and down the stairs. I could hear banging coming from the kitchen, I was sure it was Dante. As much as I tried to avoid confrontation with him, I had to go through the kitchen to get to the garage and my car. Taking a deep breath, I turned the corner and saw Dante standing at the sink. His back was to me, so I tried to slip past him. I was so close when he turned around, shooting a glare at me. "Why are you still here?"

"If you don't want me here, I'll leave, just say the word."

"It's not that. I just feel this aching loneliness. Like it's never enough." This was the most he had spoken to me in the months I'd been here.

"I don't know what you need from me."

He sighed. "I don't know either."

"When you figure it out, let me know." I shook my head as I hurried to my car.

Getting into my car, I peeled out. There was only so much I could take, and I was rushing headfirst toward that limit. He had the audacity to say he felt lonely. How that was even possible when he had men that worshipped the ground he walked on, I didn't know. He had security, and love, and all the things I craved; that all omegas craved. Yes, I was in his house, around his men, but he had never been jealous of that before. He had everything and I had nothing, no mate marks, no growly protective alphas of my own. I didn't even have security. There was nothing stopping the other omega from kicking me out on the street. The drive to work flew by as I slipped into the painful memory.

There wasn't a day that went by that I didn't regret leaving Dante and our pack behind. Not even when I was sitting across the desk from my matchmaker going through options for a new pack. One that was meant to replace the one that I had left behind, not that I wanted anyone to take their place. A beta really couldn't fill the open space that was left from leaving Dante. No alpha would be able to replace Richie. Bradley was in a class all his own, no one would ever be able to compare to him.

Fuck, I couldn't do this.

But I had to try.

Thumbing through the depressingly few folders sitting there, I couldn't help but feel like this was futile. There was nothing in those files that would tell me about the things that mattered, no indication of who they were. It was all so impersonal. That was my fault, when I had been presented with the scent cards and pack's files I hadn't been overly interested in any of them. I flipped through the folders he handed me for the third time. The first pack was mostly woodsy scents, things that made me think of a night by the campfire. There were three alphas and a beta in that one, but something in me said I wasn't a match for them. Moving that one to the back of the pile, I studied the next group. There were more alphas, too many as far as I was concerned; eight in total with such a range of scents it made my head spin. I was sure if I picked that one, I would be a match to someone. They were all so young, the oldest was a year older than my own twenty-one. I refused to be the one that broke a young pack like that.

"You don't have to pick right now." His voice made me look up at him. "You do have some wiggle room, but your heat is going to come soon, and you need to be prepared."

"No, that's not necessary." I chose one of the files at random. "This one."

"Wonderful choice. I'll have you escorted to your rooms."

Hours later I was lying in my bed staring at the ceiling. The nests they provided us with were nice enough, if a little bland. There wasn't a single touch in sight that came from me. The room was devoid of all personality, with white walls, and a large bed in the center of the wall across from the door. I had made the right decision to leave Richie, but I couldn't help but regret leaving Dante behind. He had been my best friend and confidante for so long that I couldn't stop the ache in my chest that his absence brought. I couldn't dwell on it, no, I needed to move on and make something out of my life, and that started with joining the pack I had chosen. Time would tell, but I was cautiously optimistic.

Hope was the only thing I had left to hang on to. Rejection was lethal to omegas; all I could do was hope that mine didn't kill Dante. I would never be able to forgive myself if that was the case. But I couldn't stay there, couldn't continue to act as if I had no idea. It would have destroyed me, at least this way I had a chance. It took longer than I expected for the matchmaker to return to collect me. His scent was making me nauseous as he led me through the facility. He let me walk ahead of him. A sharp pain in the back of my head is the last thing I remember from that night.

Getting to work was the easy part; dispatch was located in the center of the city, close to the prison. That should have made us feel secure, but considering the call I took this morning from my boss, that wasn't the case. There was nothing like starting your day with a phone call that tells you the man who murdered your mother had escaped. Leaving my car in the parking lot, I managed to make it inside the secured area without having a complete panic attack.

"We have live footage from Central Prison where we are following prison officials as they try to find escaped serial killer, Rhys Kelly. Mr. Kelly is most notable for the killing of one Patricia Shannon. He was ultimately convicted of ten murders but suspected of nearly three dozen." I froze in place when I heard that. There was nothing I could do to stop the pain of knowing the man who murdered my mother had escaped from prison. Ironically, it was her murder that put him in prison in the first place. And the anchor had the audacity to stand there looking bored. He couldn't even muster an ounce of compassion. As if this morning could be any worse.

Dante had made all of this nearly impossible; I missed the omega I had grown up with. The calm and compassionate, loving version of him. The man I loved and hoped to find when I came back to his house. This cold, distant version of him that I got every day was breaking my heart all over again. Trying to survive with him being so distant had been agonizing. Every time his alphas gave me even an ounce of attention, he was pouting. And they were his alphas, he had made that much clear by parading around with his marks on display, reminding me of everything I had turned my back on. It hadn't really been much of a choice to make, considering Richie was Rhys's stepbrother. That was a fun thing to discover right at the start of my first heat. But I couldn't tell anyone. Couldn't turn to the other omega I had loved since childhood. There was no help to be found in his arms when his own heat had taken him not long before. So, I had no choice but to run to Omega Services.

That led to problems of its own, leaving me in the unenviable position of choosing between never knowing if I was truly safe or biting the bullet and allowing myself to be taken in by the pack of my dreams. Omegas didn't like to share; I knew that like I knew every line to my favorite song. It didn't matter that Dante was still the same man I had grown up with. It certainly didn't matter that every time he looked at me the room flooded with his perfume. And what a delicious scent it was, mouthwatering, and so thick I could almost taste it. I craved him, and he made sure I knew he knew that. He took every chance he had been given to flaunt himself in front of me. His ass on display as he bent over, the way his shirt rode up when he reached for something on the top shelf, revealing a little bit of skin and that V line. He would shift just right and flex his shoulders in the perfect way that would have me flooded for him. And I couldn't escape it when I was with the alphas either. They loved to fantasize out loud about me and Dante. It should have bothered me. If it wasn't obvious, I liked the idea as much as they did. It was a forgone conclusion as far as I was concerned, he couldn't stand to be around me, let alone something so intimate.

But there was a part of me that hoped Dante could find space for me, prayed that we could find a happy middle ground. Either way, I couldn't focus on something I couldn't change. My head turned when I heard my mother's name on the TV. Turning it off wasn't something I could do. Especially since we kept it running at the dispatch center.

The workspace was designed to be calming for the employees. It was somewhere I could be completely in control. I loved the way the room was set up. It was a large space, broken into four pods. A long hallway broke up the rooms so everyone could get to their stations. Alphas were in the rooms closest to the door, the vents for them working at an even pace to make sure their scents stayed in that controlled area. Betas occupied the center of the space, this was more open, sharing sliding windows with both the alpha and omega rooms. The omega section was furthest into the room, the hiss of the glass wall sliding open was followed by the rush of air as the air filter kicked in. Moving to my station, I booted the computer and opened the call system. It took a moment for all the monitors to sync. There were six of them forming three giant screens. The one in the center held all the information gathering software. On the right was a map of the city with moving dots that signified where all the units were. As I took calls, the map would light up with the caller's location and the closest units. It was a nifty system that allowed us to control every second of the movements of first responders. The left-hand screen gave me direct access to the police database, allowing me to run anyone through the system for warrants and priors.

Taking a deep breath, I picked up the first call. "911, what's your emergency?"

"There's been an attack." The man's voice was full of panic.

I took a deep breath before continuing the call. "Can you tell me where you are?"

"On I-40 near exit 287"

"That's great," I mapped the call on our system, lights around it popping up, letting me know what units were available. "You said there was an attack. Can you give me more information about the nature of that attack?"

"This lady got carjacked. I think it was one of the inmates that escaped from the prison." I could hear his breathing increase to dangerous levels; there was panic in his voice when he spoke again. "She's bleeding."

I switched over to the police and fire channels, calling out to them. "Need police to respond to a carjacking on I-40."

That was how I spent my morning, answering call after call. Staying calm was easy when I knew whoever was on the other side of the line needed me. Then there were women like the one I was on the phone with right now. Her Karen was on another level.

"I'm going to go over there and say something." Her voice was beyond annoying.

"I wouldn't advise you do that ma'am."

"Why not? I'm in the neighborhood watch; it's my job to keep this neighborhood safe!"

I could already hear her moving. "Ma'am, please stay in your car, don't get out. Most importantly, those children likely live in the neighborhood. It is unnecessary for you to intervene."

"I'm going to talk to them."

I switched over to police channels. "Dispatch to RPD, I need response at the corner of Glenwood and St. Mary's, I have a Karen currently threatening children." It was a bit of an exaggeration, but it worked for me. Switching back to the call, I spoke again. "Ma'am, the police are on the way. I need you to get in the car and wait for them to arrive."

"I will do no such thing! They don't belong here."

I searched for something, anything that would distract her from what she was doing. "Ma'am, you are aware that using police to harass people is a felony? I advise you get in the car and wait for officers to arrive."

My boss tapped me on the shoulder. I looked up to see the older beta staring down at me. Putting the call on hold, I turned to her. "I have another call to this location. Reports of an adult assaulting children."

"Fuck." I jumped back to the police dispatch. "Need an ETA on your response to Karen."

"One minute."

"Make it less."

I could hear Karen arguing with me as the sirens came into hearing range. I breathed a sigh of relief. No one should have to put up with someone like her. "The cops are here, thanks for nothing."

I had never felt so relieved to end a call in my life.

Chapter 2

Dante

Watching Penelope leave for work felt like being rejected all over again. All I wanted to do was curl into a ball and cry. I didn't even feel like I could rely on my alphas anymore, they were all just as taken with her as I was. I couldn't remember the last time I had slept with my whole pack; both individually and in a cuddle pile. It was hard to go on without the very touch you had become so used to. I craved it, it had been so long. My body ached to be touched, hugged, or held. But everyone was so focused on Penelope it felt like I didn't even exist. There was something unsettling about feeling like a stranger in your own house. This wasn't even the first time it had happened.

Watching the pack move through Xavier's home was like watching a whirlwind. Wherever the older ones moved, they left a mess behind. Not that it mattered. I'd rather be in here cleaning up after them than feel so completely ignored. It was a real problem, especially since Penelope had moved to town two years ago. Having grown up with my pack around me, I was no stranger to the growing pains that came from adding to the group. But something different happened with her. It was like the moment she showed up they were laser-focused on her. And it broke my heart to realize I was slowly losing everything that I held dear. I had long ago fallen in love with my pack, my men. And now they were making a clear choice of her over me, well, all of them except Xavier.

I watched as they moved into the theatre, leaving me standing alone in the kitchen. Something had me reaching into my pocket, my thumb running over the pouch. Pulling it out, I took the chance I had to play with the items. Opening it, I collected the contents, one square at a time. The first was a piece of flannel that had once belonged to Richie, I had to cut a piece of his favorite shirt when he wasn't looking. The next was from a set of Evan's basketball shorts, the silky material between my fingers filled me with sadness, it had been too long since I spent any time with him. A square of white from one of Bradley's doctor coats; he wouldn't miss it, but it was precious to me. The satchel itself I had stolen from Xavier. Pushing the fabric back into the pouch, I shoved it into my pocket in time to catch Penelope's eyes as she came into the room. She really was the ideal omega for us, and that was the real problem. Everyone was nearly certain that she was just that, our omega. *That was the only way this would work. I had to be a beta. But there were things that made me doubt my hope. Things like that secret pouch I stuffed in my pocket.*

"Are you planning on joining us?" She came to my side, leaning into me so I had no choice but to wrap my arm around her. "You've been spending less time around us lately."

"It's nothing. I'm coming." She didn't give me time to argue, leading me into the theatre.

There was a large bed in the center of the room that the pack was spread out across. Richie called out to her, "Come on, sweetheart, I have a spot for you right here."

"I'm coming." Penelope's voice was wrapped in laughter as she pulled from my arms and went to him.

Xavier pulled me down on the edge of the bed beside him, his arms tightened around me as I buried my face in his chest. His scent surrounding me normally helped me calm the storm that was brewing in my mind. It wasn't enough this time; the fist of pain tightened in my chest as I tried to fight the tears. "What's wrong, love?" Xavier's deep voice was enough to send the tears crashing from my eyes.

"Nothing." I managed to squeak out.

"Don't start lying to me now, little one."

"Do you think I'm supposed to be a beta?"

I looked up at him in time to catch his eyes widen. "Why does that worry you?"

"I can't be our omega."

"Why not?"

I stared at him for a moment, trying to figure out if he was being real or not. "Penelope just fits that spot so much better than I do."

"How do you figure?"

"Have you not noticed the way things have changed since she joined us?" I cuddled deeper into the cave of his arms; all I wanted was to wrap myself in his scent. "She's become our center, the position that an omega is supposed to fill."

"Who said she's our omega?"

"She has to be." My heart ached at the thought of losing everyone. If we both were omegas that would tear the pack apart. I couldn't lose any of them, and that was a very real possibility. "I can't be."

"Let me see that pouch you stole from me." My eyes widened when he said that, I wasn't aware that he knew about it. My hand shook as I pulled it out and handed it to him. I couldn't watch this; I buried my face in his chest as he called out to the pack. "Pause the movie we need to talk."

"We were cuddling." Bradley's voice was like a knife through my heart.

"This is more important." I was sure everyone was looking at him from the authority in his voice. "Who do we think is our omega?"

All three of them said Penelope, but it was her voice that I wanted to hear more than anything. "I appreciate it guys, but I bet it's going to be Dante."

"You're closer to being right than any of you realize." I knew what he was doing then, as his forearms moved. "Three guesses what this is."

"Knowing Dante, it's some metal something he was working on." Bradley commented. Normally he would be right, but lately I had been feeling significantly less secure.

"You would be wrong." I could feel him moving over my head as he pulled the pieces from the pouch. "I'd wager you recognize these?"

"I don't understand." Richie's voice was closer, in fact, I could hear them all moving closer to us. "Why would he want pieces of us?"

I peeked out of the cage that was Xavier's arms so I could see Penelope as she looked down at me. There was something close to adoration there, but that couldn't be right. I held my breath, waiting for the hammer to drop. What she said made me want to kiss her. "You guys really are dense, aren't you? Can't you see what's right in front of your faces?" She spun, pushing a finger into Bradley's chest. "You of all people should know what the signs of someone becoming an omega are. Care to spell it out for us, or should I?"

"Let's see," Bradley's voice was clinical as he spoke, "when the hormones start the process the person becomes possessive over their chosen person or people."

"I'd say Dante checks that box, don't you?"

"The next thing is seeking scent marking from their packs, one or more at a time."

Penelope's eyes caught mine, making Bradley really look at me. "Pretty sure that's exactly what he's trying to do."

"Collecting clothes, pieces of their pack..."

"Go on." Penelope pressed when Bradley trailed off.

"I think you've made your point." Richie cut in. "But in all fairness those same things apply to you."

"And yet I'm the only potential omega in this pack being treated like I matter." She crossed her arms across her chest.

My heart threatened to beat out of my chest, there was no way this was going to work, but the determination in Penelope's eyes made me really want to try.

Trying to take my mind off the memory that was equal parts painful and hopeful, I went back to my sketches. There was an art to weapons designs, and since my sister left the country, I was bored. To fill the time, I started to sketch out a design for a scythe. There was something very primal about the weapon. The curve of the blade had to be just right for it to function as it was intended. Nothing was working other than this at the moment, so I needed to do anything I could to make that happen.

It felt like my world was crumbling down around me. I barely spent any time with Richie in the years before Penelope came back, now that number was as close to zero as it could get. Bradley wasn't much better with that, his eyes never stayed on me for long, especially when she came into the room. Evan was only slightly better, spending more time with me than most of the others, but it was anything but an even split. They all had made their preference clear. I could feel my pack fracturing and there was nothing I could do to keep it together, no matter how hard I tried. Xavier was my rock, the only alpha I was certain would stay with me when this all fell apart.

I was so focused on the sketch that I jumped when arms wrapped around my waist. "Someone called." I brought my head up until I was looking into his eyes. Xavier was the most traditionally attractive of my alphas. His deep brown skin danced with gold highlights as he looked down at me with cerulean eyes filled with adoration. He brushed one of his locs out of his face before speaking again. "You should probably come with."

I nodded, locking my tablet and followed him out to the car. He cranked it and we were on the way. The drive to our safe house took less time than I would have liked, leaving me little time to puzzle out what I was going to do about Penelope. There was so much wrong with what was going on I couldn't quite figure out how to fix it. It wasn't even her fault my pack was behaving this way; she did nothing wrong so I couldn't even be mad at her for it. She was always so understanding when all I wanted to do was rage. Not at her, but at my men. It was unfair that they put either of us in this position. But I had to admit, I was just as much to blame as they were. We hadn't really talked since she returned to us. If there even was an *us* anymore. The alphas were doing what alphas did, looking after the omega that needed them most. They were just so focused on her that it was starting to feel like I didn't even exist in my own home anymore.

Xavier brought the car to a stop in the woods behind the abandoned house. He got out and opened my door for me. I beamed at him as I accepted the arm he offered, letting him lead me in through the hidden door on the side of the deserted building. Slipping in was easy, but I couldn't stop thinking about the last time we were here. Xavier had his arm broken by that brute of an alpha that Calliope claimed.

My alpha noticed my hesitation, pulling me into his arms and brushing a kiss along my forehead. "I'm okay now."

"I know, I just don't like seeing you hurt."

"Well, if you had kept your hands to yourself it wouldn't have happened."

I rolled my eyes, pulling out of his arms and asking, "Since when are alphas so territorial?"

"Since always." He shook his head. "It's pretty rare that omegas grow up with their packs. It changes the way you look at things."

I shrugged and went to the desk, taking a spot perched on the edge of it and waited for Xavier to take his place behind it. That was yet another thing that had changed. When Xavier got hurt Bradley was no longer my point person. It was unacceptable that Xavier had been hurt, and I made sure everyone knew it. My alpha came around the table and took a seat there, his hand came to rest on my back, his fingers moving absentmindedly as he watched the monitor attached to the cameras. A thought crossed my mind, and before I could stop myself, I slid from where I was sitting.

Coming around, I pulled Xavier back and sat in the space under the desk. He looked down at me with a raised eyebrow. "You know the client is supposed to be here any time now."

"And?"

"I'd hate to have to kill a client for thinking he could have you."

I grinned. "Then we'll be quick."

My hands were already moving, reaching up, I pulled his zipper down, releasing his cock. My mouth watered at the sight of it. A bead sparkling at the end was too tempting to ignore. Leaning forward, I lapped at it, the taste blooming on my tongue made me take him all the way down to his knot. I gagged around him, struggling to breathe for a moment before I pulled back. I let him fall from my lips, my tongue catching his head as I licked along his length. Pulling out his balls, I lapped along them until his breath was coming in quick gasps. He was getting harder by the moment, his knot throbbing from the need to cum. Lapping at his knot made him release a deep groan. "Fuck."

I chuckled when the motion sensors started beeping. Sliding from beneath the desk I pressed a kiss to his cheek. "You might want to put your cock away. We're about to have company."

"You suck."

"We will finish at home, I promise." He growled at that.

Whatever he was going to say was cut off by the last person I expected to see coming into the room. The nearly seven-foot alpha who happened to be an escaped serial killer. "Rhys." Xavier nodded.

"You've heard I was out." There was desperation in his voice that made me way more interested.

Xavier tilted his head "A prison escape, really?"

He shrugged, "I did what was necessary to protect someone who shouldn't have even been there in the first place."

"You found your omega in prison?" I couldn't stop the surprise in my voice.

"Not mine." He denied. "He belongs to someone, got a big old bond mark."

"So that's why you're here."

He nodded. "I need something to give him to protect himself."

"If he was in prison, I'm sure he can protect himself just fine."

"He's barely bigger than you are." The desperation was back. "Please, I can't always be there to protect him."

Xavier spoke. "We will have to—"

"I have something you can give him." I cut my alpha off. I went to one of the walls where I kept some of my personal weapons. Reaching in, I grabbed two pocket daggers and a bladed set of brass knuckles. Spinning back, I approached the other alpha, closing the distance until Xavier's growl stopped me in my tracks. "Here, give these to him. He could use them more than I could, I'm sure."

He looked down at me for a moment before nodding and taking them from me. "Thank you."

Xavier was at my side, pulling me back toward the desk. "You can leave now." My alpha kept me in his arms until he was sure Rhys was gone. "Don't ever do some shit like that again."

"Like what?"

"Approach a dangerous man like that." He was bubbling right on the edge of anger, and I wanted to push him over it.

"Not like you can stop me."

His growl ripped through me, making my perfume fill the air. "I'm tempted to bend you over this desk and spank it out of you."

"You don't have the balls."

I thought he was going to burst a blood vessel when he bent me over the desk, my ass in the air. A sharp sting as he brought his hand down, "I'm," *smack* "going," *smack* "to," *smack* "make myself," *smack* "perfectly clear." My cock was rock hard as his hand impacted my cheeks. "You don't approach strange alphas." He spanked me twice more. "Do I make myself clear?"

"Yes, alpha."

"You want your alpha to fuck you, don't you?"

"I should make you wait until we get home." I hissed at him as I spun and grabbed hold of his throat. "Especially after that."

"You wouldn't dare."

"Try me." I wanted to see how far I could push this new rebellion of his. Thinking about him taking me here and now made my cock ache.

"Yellow."

I released my hold on his throat. "What's up?"

"We are treading into territory we haven't before. I think we need to discuss boundaries."

"Fair." I slid off the desk, coming around until I took the seat behind the desk.

He pulled up a chair and slid into it, facing me. "You've never been submissive with us before."

"I never wanted to." I sighed. "But something about denying you and pushing you over the edge until you just take me appeals to me."

"So, this is an experimental thing for you?"

"I think so." Even during my heats, I was dominant. Lack of control is not something I deal with well. But if I was safe with anyone it was Xavier. "I think it's you, alpha."

"Care to elaborate?"

"If I can trust anyone to keep me safe while I completely come apart, it's you."

He was beside me before I could blink, reaching out and pulling me into his arms. "I love you."

"I love you too, but what does that have to do with anything?"

"Let's go home. We can't really do this here." He took my hand and led me to the car.

Chapter 3

Xavier

We pulled into the driveway, a wicked grin came over my face when I saw there was no one else home. I was out of the driver's seat and around to his side before he got himself unbuckled. Pulling open his door, I leaned in, unlatching the belt and lifting him in one smooth motion. His laugh made my smile widen as I tossed him over my shoulder. This was one of the few things I knew for sure he loved, and he showed it by kicking his feet and giggling as I kicked the passenger door closed behind us. Getting into the house was much easier than I'd anticipated, I didn't even have to stop moving as Dante reached up and pushed the front door closed behind us. Carrying him to my room, I sat him down on the bed, taking a seat at the end of it, "Tell me what you want."

"Can we just play it by ear?"

"Red light system?"

He nodded. I was on him before he could process what was happening, tearing at his clothes until he was left with pieces of fabric hanging from his neck and limbs. The image almost made me laugh. "I liked that outfit."

"I'll buy you a new one." My voice deepened as it filled with all the promises of what I wanted to do to him.

He responded to that promise, his cock rock hard as it pressed into my stomach. My hands were already moving, stripping as quickly as I could. Collecting a blade from the bedside table, I opened it with a flick of my wrist. I needed to get rid of those scraps. He shivered as I slid the cold metal under the fabric near his neck, twisting it away from his skin as I sliced through. He stared at me with adoration clear in his eyes as I repeated the process until he was laying completely bare. Closing the blade, I set it down on the table and leaned forward to wrap my lips around his cock. I lashed out, a deep rumbling moan coming from me when the taste exploded on my tongue. His hand came down to catch the back of my head making me pull back until he fell from my lips. "Hands on the headboard."

"But, alpha." He sounded desperate.

"Be a good boy for me."

He whimpered but did as instructed. I swallowed his cock, taking my time to tease him until he was making high-pitched helpless sounds for me. He was flooding the room with his perfume as I worked him until he was begging. "Please, I need to cum."

"Not yet." His whine made me stop. "Give me a color."

He took a moment to catch his breath before he responded. "Green."

"Good boy." I leaned forward and lapped along his length. His slick was delicious as I collected it on my tongue. Flashing my eyes up to him, I winked as I swallowed the collected fluid.

"Fuck, alpha, please."

My hand slid up the inside of his thigh, my other hand reaching over him to collect the lube. Flicking it open, I wrapped my arm around his thigh so I could squeeze some out onto my waiting hand. Setting the bottle on the bed by his head, I wrapped my free hand around his length as I pushed two fingers inside him. His moan was deep and guttural as I scissored the fingers, stretching him with each motion. Sliding my hand up to his head, I teased the slit with my thumb, it was enough to make his eyes roll back in his head. "You're being such a good boy for me."

"Alpha."

"You like that don't you?" I added a third finger, rolling them up so I could massage his prostate. "It must be a relief..." My fingers moved in a small circle, I loved hearing the moans that trickled from his lips. "To know that you don't have to worry about anything..." I fucked him with my fingers, slamming the tips into him until his cock throbbed. "Because your alpha has you." I squeezed the head of his cock just hard enough to stop the cum from rushing out of it. "And I plan to ring every last bit of pleasure out of you." My voice dropped, a growl trickling into my next words, "because you are mine to please." I stroked him slowly, working him up until he was riding the edge of his orgasm. "Mine to love." I leaned forward and lapped along his head. "Mine to worship." I worked his cock and prostate in time until he was making high, desperate sounds for me. He was thrusting into my fist as I squeezed the base of him. "Mine to do what I want to. Isn't that right?"

"Please, alpha."

I worked his prostate for a moment longer; I loved to make him squirm for me. "Answer me."

"I need you, alpha." He was begging me. "I need you to knot me."

Releasing my hold on his cock, I pulled my fingers from him. "Present for me."

He came up to his knees, his head buried in a pillow. He had the most perfect ass; his cheeks were still red from the spanking I gave him earlier. That stopped me again, my hand caressed along that reddened flesh as I asked, "Did you like when I spanked you?"

"Yes, alpha." His admittance was quick.

That was all the confirmation I needed. I buried my head, lapping at his hole as it dripped for me. Working my fingers into him as slowly as I could, he moaned for me, pushing back until he was fucking himself. I loved the debauched sounds he was making as I pushed him to the brink of his orgasm. I could feel his legs starting to give out as he collapsed down on the bed, his ass shaking as he rode out the end of his orgasm. He looked so small and helpless like that, it was making me want him even more. Leaning down, I rolled him to his side, sliding in behind him.

His leg bent as I lined myself up and started to push inside him. His moan was long and high pitched as he tightened down around me. Thrusting forward until he was filled, I paused for a moment to let him adjust. My hand came around, latching onto his cock and starting to stroke him. Soon, he was pushing back against me, desperate to get more of me inside him. Moving in time with my thrusts, I glided my hand up his length, massaging the underside of his head with my thumb at every pass.

"Knot me, please, alpha," he begged.

My hand clenched down around his cock as I pushed the rest of the way inside him. His orgasm was strong and instant, tightening down around me until I was nearly feral. We exploded at the same time, his cock throbbing, cum collecting on my hand. Releasing my hold on his cock, I brought it to my lips and collected it on my tongue. A moan of satisfaction left my lips as I swallowed it.

"Fuck, alpha."

"Are you okay?" My arms tightened around him as I switched gears.

"I'm good. I promise."

"Anything you didn't like?"

He laughed. "We're still knotted together, and you want to do aftercare."

"You always do."

"That's different," he replied.

I leaned forward and nipped at his neck. "It's not, though."

"Fine, we didn't do anything I didn't like."

"Good."

"You can be less satisfied with yourself," he huffed.

"Why would I do that?"

"It's just us."

I couldn't help the laugh that came from me. "Richie always thought he would be the first one to dominate you."

"That bastard. I've got something for his ass."

I snorted. "Let's nap and we can worry about Richie later."

Chapter 4

Evan

Waiting outside of the dispatch center was not a place I liked to be. There was something inherently uncomfortable about a black ops trained mercenary sitting outside of a police station waiting for one of their omegas to leave work. Few packs could prosper with two omegas. The alphas would start to pick a favorite; it was already happening. Xavier was the only one that seemed to care about Dante, and I was incredibly thankful for that. I was still working to find a balance between them in an attempt to bring some perspective to an already tense situation. But I had always been the peacemaker. That was why betas even existed, or at least that's what I was always told by my beta parents. They hated when I joined the SEALs, didn't understand why I went AWOL as soon as I could. It took far too long for me to make that escape as far as I was concerned. Dante had been against it. He didn't get much of a choice though. The moment we started rescuing omegas was the day I started training.

We were all specialized in some way or another.

Dante was a natural tactician, and we made that work for us. Richie had the connections through his former employment at the CIA. Bradley excelled at the practice of medicine. He wasn't specialized, but I had yet to find a single thing he couldn't do, up to and including extreme life saving measures in the field. Xavier acted as Dante's bodyguard; it was a self-appointment and none of us argued with him. He was exceedingly deadly with just about anything he could get his hands on. He was also the only alpha I had ever fallen in love with.

All of these were people that Dante had come to rely on, and for the life of me I couldn't stop this pack from breaking apart around us. I needed a plan and I needed to make it fast— I couldn't let this happen. That was a pain Dante wouldn't survive. We had nearly lost him when Penelope left the first time, and I couldn't work out why she had come back at all. I needed to get to the bottom of it, and I needed to do it fast, before the damage was too great for us to repair. I can still remember the day I met this pack.

I hated transferring schools at the last minute. Halfway through senior year was the absolute worst time, and no one can argue with me about that. There was nothing like being the new senior at school. Especially when all the friend groups were already well-established. It was even harder for a beta to assimilate. I was one of the rare few that presented at sixteen, and that had begun a never-ending series of problems for me. Approaching my locker, I had to duck around a group talking in hushed tones.

I couldn't help but look over at them; a group of guys that were clustered around a smaller teen boy and girl. That was a pack if I'd ever seen one. There weren't many of them; there were two older boys, one stared at me like he was going to skin me alive for daring to look at his omegas. The other was so handsome it hurt to look at him, his blue eyes bore into me, making my heart hammer in my chest. My eyes fell the moment I realized he was an alpha. It was unusual for alphas to present early, but I knew in my heart that's what he was. There was something magnetic about him that scared me. Dropping my head, I caught the eyes of the girl, she couldn't be but maybe sixteen. She smiled at me, but there was hesitation in that gaze. My eyes moved over the smaller boy, burying my face in my locker quickly so he couldn't see the blush creeping across my face. I tried to remember what class I had next.

Biology.

That's right.

I was just reaching into the locker when I heard a whispered, "Should I go talk to him?"

There was something in that voice that made me look at the person it came from. He was much smaller than the others that surrounded him. Handsome, with dark hair and startling green eyes. There was something about him that made me want to take care of him. I couldn't focus on that though. Closing my locker, I hefted my bag over my shoulder before tossing one last look at the group.

"Hi." I jumped when I spotted those green eyes. "I'm Dante." I spun so I was facing him as he spoke to me.

"Evan."

"You're the new guy."

I didn't mean to but I rolled my eyes, "How many people transfer in at the last minute?"

"More than you'd expect. What class do you have next?"

"AP Biology."

"Me too." He babbled on as he took my hand to lead me down the hall.

I couldn't imagine what I had done to attract his attention; he was everything I had ever dreamed of. Yet, I couldn't get comfortable with him—I couldn't even tell him that I was attracted to him. My sexuality was why I had to transfer schools; the pack I was meant to be part of had fractured when they realized I was bisexual. The other boys were too interested in me, and the omega couldn't stand to be anywhere near me. Now, I just wanted to keep my head down, not attract any attention. But Dante was making that nearly impossible. Following me from class to class all day. He all but glued himself to my side. By the end of the day, he was cuddled next to me, his head resting on my shoulder as we sat staring out at the parking lot.

"You're a beta, aren't you?" There was hesitation in his voice.

"My parents are."

"You didn't answer my question."

I sighed; I hated this part. "I presented early."

"So, you are a beta...It must be nice to be so certain."

There was something in his tone that made me look down at him. "What's going on?"

"It's nothing."

He was lying to me. I didn't know how I knew but I did. "Tell me what's going on."

"It's Penelope."

"Penelope is?"

"She's the girl in my pack." He caught his bottom lip between his teeth, making me want to follow it with my tongue. "I'm pretty sure she's going to be our omega."

"I wouldn't worry too much about that if I were you. No matter who the omega for your pack is, I'm sure it's going to work out for the best."

He pulled himself tight against me when I said that, releasing a contented sigh. We were inseparable from that moment on.

Penelope chose that moment to come out from work. She really was beautiful; average size for an omega which made her slightly shorter than I was. She seemed tense. I hated that, but knew I wouldn't do a single thing to comfort her. Leaning over, I opened the door. "Such a gentleman." She tossed her hair over her shoulder. "I didn't expect you to come and get me."

"I figured we should spend some time together." I offered

"I don't know why you bother."

I pulled out onto the highway, heading toward downtown. "Why wouldn't I?"

"You never really liked me, for one."

"It wasn't that I didn't like you..."

Her laugh was a cynical one. "I know you joined the pack not long before I left. We didn't really have time to get to know each other."

"Care to tell me why you left?"

"I fail to see how that's any of your business." She sounded over it.

I pulled onto a side street slamming the car into park as I spun on her. "It's my business because your leaving almost killed Dante. I had to see the man I love more than anything fall apart and nearly starve to death because *you* rejected him. So give me a good reason not to drop your ass somewhere and pretend you disappeared."

"Fine," she huffed, "I don't know what I'm doing here anymore than you do. I just needed somewhere to recover before I moved on with my life. I certainly didn't expect to be staring down my heat and still be around my pack...this pack. You know what I mean."

"I do know what you mean."

"And I can't even say anything to anyone because Dante comes first, he always should." She was so self-sacrificing it was infuriating.

"Have you ever thought you should be a little more honest with everyone? Stop being so closed off, especially with Dante. This isn't getting any easier on any of us, and you are the only one that can do anything to change that."

"I...I don't know if I can."

"Then walk the fuck away, and don't come back this time." I put the car into gear and peeled off.

Chapter 5

Rhys

A week after I left the weapons maker, Liam and I drove around for a few hours before hunkering down for the day in an abandoned house. As we hid there, we started to talk to each other like it was the most natural thing for us to do. "So, you told me all about that alpha that marked you. Now tell me why you were in prison."

He hesitated. "You aren't going to believe me."

That made me laugh. "Try me."

"What would you say if I told you I was part of a covert operation to take down some of the worst human-trafficking rings in existence?"

"I've heard stranger things." I stared at him. "Go on."

"My alpha and I are... well, *were* DEA and NCIS, respectively."

"So, you're a cop." I crossed my arms over my chest. I was debating wrapping my hands around his neck and strangling the life out of him. "Then why were you in prison?"

"I killed the wrong person."

"Care to elaborate?"

He sighed. "My job was to go undercover. There was a plan for me to be sold into one of the groups we were targeting. The night my alpha marked me, he took me to auction. It was days ahead of schedule, but he did what he thought was best. I've killed more people than I care to admit over the years."

"Years?! How long were you under?"

"Seven years. It wasn't supposed to be that long, but I was traded." He looked at the ground as he answered me. "They lost me."

"What do you mean they lost you?"

"Things constantly shift when you're being sold. It can be easy to get lost in the shuffle." He shrugged.

"So, you killed the wrong person?"

"Yeah, I got too close to one of the men who had me, and when I killed his boss, he pulled some strings."

Night had fallen while we spoke, so I made a split-second decision that I hoped didn't come to bite me in the ass. "Come on, let's get you somewhere safe."

We took the car I had stolen, and he directed me to one of the safehouses he knew about in the middle of the forest, outside the city. Moving was a tricky thing, but I couldn't risk this omega falling into the wrong hands, or worse yet, back in prison. I shouldn't have cared, but I did. Getting to the cabin, I left him in the car as I went to check inside. I didn't know why I felt the need to get this omega back to his alpha, his pack, but I did. I flicked on lights as I passed, looking in closets as I came across them. There was nothing I could do about the sparse conditions, but I could make sure there was no one else inside. Liam studied me as I waited for him to get inside, everything in me was telling me that he needed to be safe.

Coming back outside, I waved him in. His movements were rushed as he jumped out of the car, nearly slamming the door behind him and scrambling into the cabin. I spent half an hour getting him settled in before I was ready to head out. When I pulled the door closed behind me, I heard him slamming the dead bolt into place. That simple sound made relief flood me in a way I never expected. With that, I turned and headed to the car.

Sliding into the driver's seat, I started it and aimed toward the city. I had a hit list and I needed to start checking them off. My initial stop was the house of the first woman who testified against me in court. She survived one of my more brutal attacks and was the reason I was sentenced to solitary confinement. Pulling into her neighborhood, I grinned when I saw her house was isolated from the road and her neighbors. I scanned the surrounding area before deciding to park further away, up the block. I would steal one of her pack member's cars to get out of here.

They hadn't moved after I killed here. No, she was currently living here with her pack and their two kids. It paid to have people on the outside that owed you, and the ones that owed me made sure I had everything I needed. That included the locations of all my targets. This was the first, but there would be more to come, rest assured at that. Coming around the side of the house I opened the gate into the backyard and went to the nursery window, which opened when I pulled on it. Sliding into the house, I smiled when I saw that the child was alone there.

I reached into my other pocket and pulled out the spool of metal. Slipping the leather gloves I was holding onto my hands, I started to unspool that wire. Taking my time, I prepared my deadly trap, feeling much like a spider as I laid the web of metal out. I had a pattern; a signature is what they called it. I wasn't all that ashamed of it, if I'm honest, since I tended to target child abusers. There were a lot more of those than people wanted to admit, and that victim pool overlapped with police officers too often for anyone to be comfortable with. I should have passed this one's mother over—should have stopped myself from going after yet another cop. But the way she looked at her children was disgusting. The way she spoke to them was even worse. It was the pack's alpha I was here to kill tonight. I felt no guilt at that thought. Alphas were the most dangerous of the designations, it didn't take much to push one of us to violence.

I was just finishing up when I heard a car pull up in the driveway. That was my cue. I slid back down the hall and into the nursery. Cradling the child in my arms, I climbed back out through the window and went around the house back to the front door. Shifting the baby into one arm, I pulled the small revolver from my pocket. Ringing the doorbell, I slid the gun beneath the blankets and waited. It didn't take long for someone to open that door. The younger man started to speak, but froze when he saw me holding the child.

"Let me in and she doesn't get hurt." It wasn't a threat, but it was close. The beta folded, moving to the side to allow me entrance. He hesitated; I knew he was about to call for help. I silenced him by shoving the pistol into his back. He started to move, allowing me to kick the door closed behind me.

"Who was that, love?" The woman's voice made an evil grin spread across my face. She was why I was here anyway; it was ultimately her fault this was happening.

Bringing my arm back, I slammed the butt of the gun into the beta's head before turning it on the female alpha. "Reach behind the sofa and tie your pack up." She started to run, but I turned the gun back on the child in my arms. "Do as you were told."

Standing over the beta, it was all I could do not to laugh at how easy he had made it to get into his house. There was nothing he could do to stop me from killing him and everyone inside. Not that I was here for any of them, no, that prize belonged to the woman of the house. An alpha this time, lot of good it did. The baby in my arms was silent and that should have been more alarming to its parents than anything. They were calm, but then, they had no idea what I had planned for their woman.

She was making quick work of tying the rest of her pack up, making them easy for me to ignore. I caught the look she gave me, and I shook my head. "Don't fuck around with me," I pulled the blanket back, exposing the pistol I held pointed at the baby's chest. "Tighter, we don't want them interrupting us, now do we?"

She shot me a gaze meant to be a challenge. "I don't know what you want."

"You really expect me to believe you don't know who I am?"

"I assure you, I don't."

"See, I would believe you," I moved to the table in the center of the living room, pulling out a wallet from her purse. With a flip of my wrist, I opened it to the shield inside, "but I know for a fact a homicide detective like you knows exactly who and what I am. Seems like you followed in your mommy's footsteps."

"Cop killer."

"You say that as if it's an insult." Stepping back, I set the wallet on the table. Moving to the opposite side of the room, I set the infant in the play pen, taking the pistol in my hand and turning back to the alpha. She started to move, coming up to her feet and charging at me. I took a quick step to the right, so I was in front of the play pen. "I wouldn't do that if I were you."

"I'm not doing a thing you say."

Her snarl was almost cute. "You are fully aware that children are simply a tool I use to get into the house. They are never hurt."

"That makes it an empty threat."

"It's cute you think my unwillingness to kill a child, a literal infant, makes my threat empty." I sighed. "Behave or I make your baby an orphan."

That stilled her. It was all part of my plan, my pattern, break into the nursery, that was the easy part. Cops were so over-confident in their ability to protect their packs; so much so they rarely had alarms, making them easy targets. The irony of it made me laugh... It didn't take long for their babies to get used to me until I was coming and going as I pleased.

She was just like her mother in that regard, thinking that with me behind bars she was safe from anyone who might want to hurt her. It made her all the more vulnerable. Her child was too trusting of strangers, just like she had been. It felt fitting to me that she die the same way her mother did. Pushing the gun into the small of her back, I forced her down the hall to the nest. She turned around, hesitating just inside the door, frozen in place. I knew what she was seeing; the silver thread was spun so razor thin it would tear at her ankles as she moved. The same threads were spread across the bed so when she made it there, they would cut her in so many places she would eventually die in agony. Just the way I liked it. I drank their pain and fear like fine wine, savoring their pained sounds and begging. Just like I would do to this one. My hand came up, catching the back of her neck. I tossed her toward the bed, watching as blood dotted the ground with each step. I loved seeing each drop blossom as it hit the hardwood floor.

She was quiet, seeming to take the pain in stride. She was likely planning her escape, but there would be none. My preparation of the room left her with no choice but to obey me or die. Well, she would die regardless. I sincerely hoped she didn't choose the easy option. It would be disappointing as hell for my first murder in twenty years to be so simple and inelegant. She stopped again looking down at the bed as if trying to find a position that would cause the least amount of damage. I didn't care what she wanted, spinning her around until she was looking up at me.

Pushing her back, I reveled at the sound of her scream as she hit the bed. Using my free hand, I pulled my phone out of my pocket. "911 what is your emergency?"

"I'm afraid I've committed another murder."

There was furious typing on the other side of the phone. "You said another?"

"That's correct."

"How many others have you committed?" She was fishing and I allowed it.

"The actual number and what I was convicted of are two vastly different sums."

Her sharp inhalation made me smile. "Rhys, you could do us all a favor and turn yourself in."

"We both know that isn't happening."

"Whose body are we recovering this time?" I knew what she was doing with all those key clicks, each of them triangulating the phone, trying to get a bead on my location.

"As if I've ever told anyone that before."

She sighed, "So why did you call us?"

"Someone needs to untie the rest of the pack so they can care for the child." There was silence for a moment, my brain filling in what she was doing like I was there. She had likely switched over to connect with the police coming to the house. "You might want to tell them to hurry. The detective here isn't lasting as long as the others."

"There isn't anything I can say to stop this, is there?"

She wasn't talking to me, but I heard it over the open line. "There isn't...It just occurred to me, you never gave me your name."

"Penelope."

She was unsure of herself for the first time since this conversation started. "Penelope... I killed someone who had a daughter named Penelope. One Sergent Shannon. Any relation?"

The line went silent for a moment before an older woman came over the speaker. "Tell me why you kill, Rhys."

"Put Penelope back on the line and I just might. Otherwise, I'll just open the detective's throat and maybe kill the rest of her pack on the way out."

More silence before Penelope was back. "So, you killed my mother."

"It certainly would've been stupid for me to confess if I didn't kill the bitch."

"What did she ever do to you?" That was hissed through the speaker by a woman who was barely biting her tongue.

"Got too close to catching me in the act." I would never tell her the real reason I had targeted her mother. She was the only person that was safe from me. The only truly innocent one in this whole thing. Something in me was screaming to make her mine and I was inclined to listen, I just needed to find a way to do it.

My next thought was cut off by the sound of sirens coming up the driveway. "We can pick this up next time."

I left the call open, tossing the phone onto the bed before I pulled open the window and climbed out. Lowering myself down was much easier with the muscle I put on in prison. The drop to the ground wasn't enough to do more than slightly wind me before I was up and running, climbing over the fences to adjoining streets. I jumped back into my car and steered it toward the safe house Liam was hiding in. I would spend one more night there with him before moving on. By then, I would be sure that he was safe and would have figured out a way to get in contact with his alpha.

Chapter 6

Penelope

I was told to go home by my supervisor, department policy, apparently. Not that I wanted to go home. I would much rather be anywhere but in the house with Dante. I couldn't take the pain in his eyes when he looked at me any longer than I had to. That led me to walking down the street to the domestic violence shelter. There wasn't much that I could do about the situation with Dante, but there was a lot I could do to help people like me.

Omega victims of alphas.

The chime above the door rang as I pushed it open, "Come around the desk, I'll be out there in a minute."

"Take your time." I called out to Amani, the beta that ran the shelter, and Xavier's missing little sister. That was a little tidbit I was keeping to myself. It wasn't my secret to tell.

Going to the computer there, I started to pull up the inventory to find out what they were short on. They were usually low on blankets and pillows, and the log showed as much. Making a list as I went, I worked my way through the data while I waited for Amani to finish up and join me. I wasn't trying to listen to what they were saying but I couldn't help myself. There was something about her tone when she addressed the alpha that made my skin crawl.

"I don't give a damn if you're the pope or the chief of police. There is nothing you can say to me that will force me to violate client confidentiality." That was the key phrase I had been waiting on.

Leaning over, I spotted Dorian, the only alpha on staff, and the security guard. "Hey, alpha, Amani needs some help in there."

"There are things I can do to you that will make you wish you gave me what I asked for." The rage in the man's voice pissed me off.

I turned the corner, charging into the room. It took me less than a moment to assess who was there. An alpha stood between me and Amani and there was a beta sitting in front of her. I was moving before anyone could react, catching the alpha with a heel to his knee. That made him crumble to the ground, my fist finding the side of his head as blood started welling on the carpet beneath him. I had the beta in a chokehold dragging him back out of the office by the time Dorian made it into the room. I nearly threw the beta at him, going to Amani.

"Are you okay?" She waved me off.

"I'm fine." Crossing the room, we watched as Dorain drug both men from the room. She pulled the door closed behind her, taking a cigarette from the case in her pocket and lighting one of them. Tobacco and marijuana smoke filled the air as she tried to calm her nerves. "That happens twice a week." Watching her hazel eyes move around the room made me smile, it was just so normal for her to be hypervigilant in her line of work. That normalcy was exactly what I needed right now. She reached up and played with one of the dark brown curls that filtered down around her face; there was something different about her that I couldn't quite place.

"Let me hit that." I tried to pull the joint from her grasp.

She swatted me away with a manicured hand. "Get your own."

"Fine." I slid past her, pulling out her extra case and lighting one of my own. "I've had a day."

"You're not the only one." She took a seat across from me, leaning against the desk. "How's life at Casa Dante?"

"Awkward." I sighed. "Your brother isn't making life any easier."

"I left for a reason."

"I've never asked."

"That makes me want to tell you." It felt like an admission that was torn from her soul.

"I'm all ears."

"You have to understand there aren't many people like us around anymore." I didn't know what to say to that. "Royal packs, I mean. The myths are more like histories if I'm being honest. When humans evolved into what we are now, there were betas, then alphas, and finally, omegas. The first alphas and omegas were the royals. One hundred alphas in total and only twenty-five omegas. Xavier and I are direct descendants of one of the first packs."

"Like Ayden." It wasn't a question; Ayden was Calliope's alpha.

"Yes, like Ayden." Her smile made me relax against the chair. "How is Calliope?"

"She's fine as far as I know. They haven't been in contact much considering the whole pack is running from the law."

"She made a lot of women feel safe on these streets. It's unfortunate she isn't here anymore." That made me smile. Amani was one of the few outside Calliope's pack that knew she was a serial killer.

"Someone else will step into her shoes, I'm sure of it."

She took a long drag from the spliff before changing the subject. "When a royal omega has children they only have alphas and omegas."

"I don't understand."

"I know you don't. I can't even grasp it. Here I am, a beta with a royal omega for a mother." The smoke curled in the air as she exhaled. "According to Mom, a royal beta is just an omega that hasn't presented yet."

"But you're nearly thirty."

"I'm twenty-eight, thank you."

I grinned, knowing I had hit a nerve. "Twenty-eight, fine. I know some omegas present late, but that's like twenty-four, twenty-six at the latest."

"Supposedly, a royal omega only presents when she finds the right alphas."

I thought about that for a while, trying to think of what I could do to help her. "Okay, so we find out."

"Find out?"

"Yeah, I can reach out to someone at omega services. They have matchmakers that specialize in discreet matches."

"We both know all too well what matchmakers they have." She sat back in the chair, her eyes falling closed. "Even if I agreed, what would it accomplish?"

"You get a pack to love and care for you."

She rolled her eyes. "I'm not an omega."

"And this can prove just that to your parents."

"I'm going to tell you something, but you have to promise not to say a word to anyone." She caught my eyes for a long moment waiting for me to nod. When I did, she tossed her hair over her shoulder, exposing the mark on her throat that I was certain belonged to Dorian. "I'm not really a beta anymore. Turns out the royal legends are true."

"You're on suppressants."

She smiled. "Nope."

"An alpha, really?"

"Don't sound so doubtful," she chided me.

"When?"

"It's relatively recent. I wish I had more to tell you, but it's kind of still developing." She caught Dorian's eye over my shoulder.

Wonderful. "None of that tells me why you don't want Xavier knowing where you are."

"I love my brother, but he was everything my parents wanted him to be. That was, until it became obvious that Dante was his mate."

"They really didn't want him with Dante, did they?"

She stared at me for a moment, her lips turning into a smile. "I think they hoped you and him would hit it off."

"He's gay."

"I know that, you know that, hell, my parents know that." Her laugh was a cynical one. "But they couldn't seem to grasp the truth in front of their eyes."

"They must have lost it when Dante showed up with Xavier's mark."

A smile spread across her face. "It was funny to watch, I'm not going to lie. They moved on pretty quickly to me. At that point, I was a beta, Mom was sure I was going to be an omega. She found a pack for me and everything."

"Why?"

"Arranged matings aren't as uncommon in the royal communities as you might think. That's what the matchmakers are for." She shook her head. "But I'm lecturing. They want grandkids, but all parents do."

"I wouldn't know," I sighed. When my mom was murdered, her pack followed her quickly. That was the thing the media never talked about. When a pack's omega dies, the whole pack tends to follow them. In the unfortunate instance where an alpha is killed, the omega will likely commit suicide. That was what it was like for my parents' pack. When my alpha mother was murdered, her omega followed quickly after. The rest of the pack didn't think for one second about the omega child they were leaving alone in this world. Taking a deep breath, I looked up at Amani and forced a smile. "But I understand that's a normal thing parents want."

"I can't let them know about Daniella." She was talking about her daughter, an adorable five-year-old girl who was the spitting image of her mother, with the same tightly coiled hair. Just then, there was a commotion outside the office that Amani hurriedly went to tend to. I took that opportunity to sneak out and head back to Dante's house.

Chapter 7

Evan

I couldn't sit by and watch Dante drift away from us. And that was something we were in danger of, considering the way the alphas had been treating him lately. That was why I had a date night planned for us. Xavier would be around later to collect Dante for their night, but now was our time, and I had the perfect thing arranged. He was in the passenger seat, his eyes scanning the road as I drove us through the city. "Where are you taking me?"

"It's a surprise."

"You know I hate those." He was just a hair's breadth away from releasing his whine.

"Don't bother, it doesn't hit me like it does the alphas."

He crossed his arms over his chest with a huff that I couldn't help but find adorable. "Fine, but it better be good."

Twenty minutes later we were pulling into the parking lot. There was something beautiful about watching Dante as he took in the Harleys parked outside the tattoo parlor. Watching him put everything together was a wondrous thing, he seemed entranced as he tracked the comings and goings of the MC that ran the place. I couldn't tell if he was excited or nervous. Either way, I knew he was going to love my gift to him. I got out of the car, coming around to open the door for my omega. He took the hand I offered him, letting me lead him into the parlor.

"Welcome to Demon's Run Tattoos," the female alpha behind the counter called out to us. "If you don't mind filling out these consent sheets, I can get started on your designs."

"Thanks, Delilah," I said to the woman as I collected them from her before leading Dante to the seats in the makeshift waiting area. "Do me a favor and don't look at the design I came up with for you."

"It's not something I'm going to hate, is it?"

"Would I do that to you?" I was teasing him.

"Considering how everyone else has been acting..."

"Fair enough." I reached over to ruffle his hair. "But I'm not everyone else, and neither is Xavier."

He smiled at me before filling out the paperwork. I filled mine out and collected them, taking the forms back to the counter. "If you'll follow me." I waited for Dante while she led us to the back of the parlor and her chair. She raised her eyebrows at me. "Okay, who's first?"

"I'll go first," I answered.

"Great." She turned back to lay out the stencil. "If you'll take off your shirt, we can get started."

I pulled it over my head, handing it to Dante. His eyes widened as he studied my chest. I wondered if he was imagining all the naughty things I do to him. Delilah took her time, making sure the placement was perfect before she started. The buzz of the machine cut through the silence as I waited for the first bite of pain. It came quickly, followed by the burning of her dragging the needle across my skin. I let myself drift off to the place the pain created, somewhere between agony and bliss. It was just enough to keep my mind from wandering too much, but not enough to dull the one memory that surfaced.

Tonight was much like any other night; we were spending the night at Dante and Calliope's house. Dante's room was the largest, allowing the whole pack to crowd into the space. There was something off tonight, but I couldn't quite put a finger on what it was. The alphas were busying themselves in the kitchen, taking care of making the food for the rest of us. Penelope disappeared around the corner, leaving me alone with Dante. This was a rare thing, and I cherished every moment I had with him.

"Come here." I opened my arms to him, he crawled across the bed, wrapping himself around me.

"Can I ask you something?"

His voice was small, making me look down at him with concern. "Anything."

"How would you feel if I was an omega?"

"I don't care what your designation is, I fell in love with you, not your biology."

He buried his face in my chest, inhaling deeply before releasing a satisfied sigh. "I believe you."

"What brought this up?

"Nothing." He shook his head.

"What did I tell you about lying to me?" I kept him boxed in with my arms as I waited for him to explain.

"Have you noticed the difference in the way they treat me?"

"You mean since I..." I shot my eyes down the hall in the time to catch Penelope peeking out at me from the living room, "Joined the group? I don't know if I'm the best person to ask. Some of the others have been here much longer than I have."

"I don't know if it's jealousy, but I feel out of place now. Like she's replacing me."

"No one can replace you." I caught his chin between my fingers, bringing his face up. Seeing that doubt in his eyes was breaking my heart. "You are everything I've ever dreamed of having. Beta, omega, none of that matters. I love you for you."

"You love me?"

That light was back in his eyes; I would do anything to keep it there. "More than anything, watching you doubt your place here is breaking my heart."

He studied me for a moment, looking much younger than his seventeen years. I pulled him into my arms, his head coming to rest against my chest. "There's nothing that could happen that would take me from you. Not a single thing that anyone could say that would make me doubt your place in my life. I couldn't care less if you were our omega, or a beta like me. All that matters is your happiness, there isn't a thing anyone could do to change that for me. I love everything about you."

"Even if I'm our omega?"

"Especially then." I longed to chase that ache from his voice. "I can't wait until I can officially make you mine. It hasn't been long, I know that, but I know you are mine as well as I know every word to my favorite song. Nothing, and I mean nothing, *will change that."*

"All done." Delilah's voice pulled me out of that memory rather quickly. I sat up on the chair before getting to my feet and going over to the mirror. Raising my right arm over my head, I studied the completed tattoo. It ran the length of my side, stylized roses filling in the region beside a blocky script that read 'Dante's beta'. I beamed seeing the clear branding on my skin. "Your turn."

She was calling for Dante; this was where I came in. "Love, I have another request for you."

"What's that?"

I produced a silk blindfold from behind me. "Put this on?"

Dante

I was startled by Evan's request for a moment. There was no way he was asking me to be so vulnerable in a strange place surrounded by new people. But I couldn't stop the thrill that went through me at the thought of putting myself completely in his hands. I reached my hand out to take the piece of fabric from him. Placing it across my eyes, I felt hands on me, Evan's, guiding me to the chair. He tugged on my shirt until it disappeared over my head. Every touch as someone put the stencil on seemed intensified without my sight. The buzz of the machine as it turned on made me jump. I tensed for a moment until warm hands found my chest, followed by the bite of the needle. There is nothing quite like the feeling of being tattooed, it provided a sense of clarity I had been sorely missing.

The pain was making me react in the most unexpected way, my cock growing hard in my pants, pressing against my zipper in a nearly painful way. I shifted in the seat, trying to find some relief. I realized I failed when the machine cut off, followed by cool liquid on my chest as they cleaned the tattoo. Their hand moved down my body, thumb teasing the head of my cock. "Hey!"

"It's me." Evan's voice in my ear made me relax.

"But what about everyone else?"

"We're alone." His hand slid into my pants, wrapping around my cock and stroking the length slowly. My hands tightened around the arms of the chair, the feeling of his fingers moving as he stroked me was driving me insane. "You're being such a good boy for me." He ran his thumb along the underside of my head, collecting the slick that lay there. His moan made me throb for him. "Fuck, you taste so good."

I heard his zipper and felt his weight on top of me as he seated himself. He reached between us, lining my cock up with his hole and sitting all the way down until I was buried. "You're so tight," I strangled out.

"Hold still." His words froze me in place. I throbbed inside him as the buzz started again. The pain of the needle against my skin made me ache to move, long to touch him, but I couldn't risk distracting him . His progress was slow as he worked the gun. I needed him to hurry up and finish. Reaching out, I wrapped my hand around his cock, stroking him slowly so he was being as tortured as I was. His cock was leaking for me, his precum making my thumb slide over his head in a most satisfying way. He moaned for me, bucking against my hold as I teased him. "You're a sneaky omega, aren't you?"

"Hurry up and finish so I can fuck you right."

The buzzing cut off then as he shifted in my lap. "It's done."

My hips started to move as soon as he said that, pounding into him as he moaned for me. He had kept me on the edge for too long, it didn't take much time until I exploded inside him.

My head snapped to the side as I heard a noise, followed by a feminine laugh and a muffled, "Sorry."

"Let me get that off of you."

I was blinded for a moment as he pulled the silk from my eyes. His weight shifted on my lap making me reach out and stop him. "I just need a moment."

He shifted a little, sending me bucking in the chair. I was about to curse him when he pulled the blindfold off. It took me long moments for my eyes to adjust to the light, when they did, I looked up into Evan's eyes. There was a hint of mischief that made me look down, at chest height he was holding a small mirror. Gazing into it, I started beaming when I spotted the watercolor orchids sitting just below my collar bone, elegant script along the bottom read, 'Evan's Omega'.

Chapter 8

Bradley

I loved to watch Dante work. He was most himself when he was at a forge, a large hammer in his hand while the clanging of metal against metal as he pounded out his frustrations rang out. He hated being out of control. There was something about it that made him volatile. Like now, he tossed the mallet toward a wall, making me have to duck quickly to avoid getting smacked in the head with it. "Could you not? I'd sure hate to ruin this pretty face."

"Then stay the fuck out of my way," he snapped, grabbing a glob of metal and adding it to the end of the blade he was building. He was rage-smithing, and I wasn't sure if I wanted him to work it out or fuck it out. Both ideas had their merits. He ultimately decided for me, snarling , "Just get the fuck out."

Shaking my head, I closed the door behind me as I slid into the hallway. Evan passed me as I was coming out; I stopped him with a hand on his arm. "Dante's in a mood."

"He should be." The beta pulled away from me in a huff and went into the smithy.

Everything was going to shit, and I was scrambling to put it all back together. And I was failing miserably. I really just wanted things to go back to the way they were when we were kids. I couldn't stop thinking about the last time we had both omegas.

"Alpha, I need to ask you something." Dante's voice made me turn to look at him.

I couldn't help but smile at him, freshly eighteen and finally designation tested. I welled with pride knowing that they both were mine. They were the youngest of us, but we were close to each other in age; less than seven years between Dante and me. My hand came up, brushing an errant hair from his eyes. "What's that?"

"Do you ever wish you could have just Penelope?"

"Never." My reaction was instant and guttural. The thought of not having Dante made me rage. "There is nothing that could happen that would make me not want you. I've loved you for as long as I can remember."

"Even if you have to choose between me and Penelope?"

That stopped me, making me turn and look at him. "Love, why would I have to choose between you two?"

"She's supposed to be our omega." He looked up at me with doubt glistening in his eyes. "I was meant to be a beta. You all have always treated me like a beta."

"Come here."

I held my arms out to him, he filled them easily, letting me bury my nose in his hair. "I can't lose you guys."

"We aren't going anywhere, love." I pressed a kiss to his forehead. "That much I can promise you."

"You can't promise me that."

"The fuck I can't," I snarled. "The world would have to explode for me to not be at your side."

"I got the call from Omega Services."

It felt like he dropped a bomb on top of my head. His scent shifted enough to make me ache to make him mine. "Well, then you're our omega."

"It would seem that way."

"Why don't you sound happy about that?" There was a sadness in his voice that I needed to get to the bottom of.

"Packs can't exist with two omegas."

"Who said that?"

"Biology."

"You know, one of the things they teach you in medical school is the evolution of our species." He was clinging to me like I was the last port in the storm his emotions created. "At one point, we lived in communal housing where omegas were celebrated, the most important members."

"What happened?"

I knew I had him then. "What always happens, little one. Others, mostly alphas, decided that since there were more of them than omegas, that they should decide." His eyes sparkled as I spoke, "Society is only as strong as its weakest members, and through centuries of brainwashing, we have come to believe that omegas are the weakest of us."

"But we are."

"Physically, omegas may be, but not everything has to be physical. Omegas are meant to be our leaders, the ones we look to for comfort, love, and guidance. Alphas have come to take that for granted, taking everything they can from their omega and giving nothing in return."

"But you're an alpha, and you aren't like that."

I smiled down at him. "You know that, but not everyone does. It's better to go out of your way to show you aren't a threat than it is to make anyone feel uncomfortable."

"What does that have to do with me?"

"You're our omega, I don't plan on treating you as anything but precious."

Yeah, I was fucking this up at every turn. I couldn't remember the last time I had held Dante as we slept, let alone the last time we kissed. No wonder he was mad at me. Xavier was sitting in the kitchen when I came out. He looked at me with a contempt in his eyes that echoed what I so acutely felt. "I'm going out."

He nodded, leaving me to make a mad dash to the car. There was only one thing that I could do to make this up to him. The cell phone was already in my hand as I called the one person I knew would help me fix this. It was ringing as I put it to my ear. "This had better be important for you to be calling my omega."

Ayden had every right to be pissed at me; it was unusual for an alpha to call a mated omega. "Can you put Calliope on? I need to talk to her."

"What the fuck are you thinking?" Calliope's voice came over the speaker. "How dare you make Dante feel like a stranger in his own house. If I had known letting you take Penelope in would result in this, I would have figured something else out. And don't you think for one second I won't bring my ass back there and slaughter you where you stand."

"I know."

"You know?!" she snapped. "You don't know a thing. Did you know he's been crying himself to sleep for the last month?"

"I didn't."

"How about that he hasn't slept in his own fucking bed since she's been in the house?"

"I knew that."

"And you didn't think that was strange at all?" she continued before I could respond. "Don't answer that." I could hear her cursing and I knew she was just getting started. "Why have you and Richie not spent even a single second with Dante in the last six months?"

"I help him in his smithy every day."

That sounded defensive, even to me. "Have you actually had a conversation with him?"

"Not in a while." I hated admitting that.

"Why aren't you doing exactly that?"

"Because he threw a mallet at my head and kicked me out."

"You aren't home, are you?" She was frighteningly calm.

"I'm not."

"Then take your ass back there and talk to your omega." Silence was the only thing that greeted me after that.

The wheels squealed as I turned the car around and headed back to the house. Years ago, I had promised him I would never make him doubt his place in my life. I had done just that by focusing all my attention on Penelope. I thought I was doing the right thing. Was convinced she needed me more than Dante did. Now I saw how stupid that was.

Pulling back into the driveway, I was in the house before the car settled. Dante and Xavier were sitting at the table, their conversation ending as soon as I came in. "Dante," my voice shook, "Can we talk?"

"Fine." He was cold, it was my own fault. I had long neglected my omega.

I started to head toward the nest, before stopping and taking a seat at the table with them. "I've really fucked this up, haven't I?"

Dante rolled his eyes. "That's the understatement of the year."

I sighed, "Tell me how to fix this."

"You shouldn't have to be told how to care for your omega." Xavier was too calm.

I nodded, trying to find the words. Reaching for Dante, I nearly cried when he pulled his hand away from mine. "Do you want me to leave?"

"No!" There was panic in his eyes as he grabbed my hand. "Don't leave, that will just make it worse."

"What do you need from me?"

"Grovel." I grinned, that wouldn't be all that hard.

One Week Later

"Where are we going?" Annoyed Dante was the cutest thing ever.

There was amusement in my voice. "I'm groveling."

He huffed, turning his head and staring out the window. Trees zipped past us as we pulled onto the bridge that would take us over Jordan Lake. The reflection of the sun off the water was enough to make Dante's eyes dart along its surface. I knew he would be trying to figure out where we were, where we were going. Not that he would be able to, there wasn't anything around us that would tell him anything. Where I was taking him wasn't on anyone's radar, it was relatively new and word hadn't gotten around yet. He was studying the area as I pulled from the bridge onto a side road. He had been so excited when we left the house, our bond was nearly screaming from it, now he was shut down again. I was sure when we got there all of that would change.

"Seriously, we've been driving forever. Where are we going?" He was getting more annoyed by the moment, and I loved it.

"It's been twenty minutes. And we're almost there."

"I just want to go..." His words cut off as I pulled into the parking lot. I could see his eyes moving as he took in the sheets of metal laying on their side while I parked in front of the doors. Dante seemed too stunned to speak.

"Still want to go home?"

"Take me home now and I'll never forgive you."

"So, I'm forgiven?" I couldn't help but tease him.

"Not yet." He turned and finally gave me his full attention. "But you're getting there."

I got out of the car, satisfaction brimming as I ran around to get his door for him. Holding my arm out to him, he took it, sliding up against me. "Good boy."

"Welcome." The beta approached me with his hand out. "You must be Dante."

"You must be stupid," Dante snapped.

"Be nice," I whispered into the omega's ear. "I'm sorry about that." I turned to the salesman. "I'm Bradley, and I wouldn't know one metal from another."

"I'm Dante." My omega cut in. "The one that will be making the purchases today. You would do well to remember that if you want what is sure to be a massive commission."

"I thought..."

"You thought wrong." Dante cut him off. "Now, I don't suppose you have any other salesman here, do you?"

"I assure you that I'm more than capable of helping you myself."

"You aren't capable of holding your breath if it would save your life." Dante's whisper had me stifling a laugh at the beta's expense. To the man, my omega continued. "I am sure there is literally anyone but you that could help us."

"Forgive me," a woman's voice cut into the conversation, "I couldn't help but overhear, and I'm sure that I can help you with whatever you need."

We turned as one, facing her. She was small, not much bigger than Dante. She reminded me so strongly of my mother that I was frozen for a moment. "Siobhan," I called out to my cousin, "I haven't seen you in forever."

"It hasn't been that long." Her smile warmed my heart. "I only married Shannon O'Doyle two years ago."

"It's been longer than that. How has the Irish Mafia been treating you?"

"Well enough to open my own metal shop."

"I should have known. W ho else would name their business Irish Rose Metal?"

"This is my sale." The beta looked pissed.

"It's my business, and you can't disrespect customers, especially ones that are family." She all but dismissed him before turning back to us. "What can I get for you?"

Dante seemed so sure of himself. "I think I'd like to start with the titanium."

Siobhan smiled over at me. "Wonderful, if you two will just follow me, we can get started."

Twenty minutes later, I was walking the aisles behind Dante as Siobhan was explaining the purity of their metals. "It all depends on what you get. Precious metals, we have everything from 24 karat down. With steel, it depends on the composition you want."

"Forgive me if I test that myself." Dante was more focused on the metal than he was Siobhan.

I leaned down and whispered in his ear, "Be nice." I offered her a gentle smile.

"Can we please have some time? I prefer to shop alone."

"Are you sure?" Siobhan hesitated, "I'd be more than happy to show you anything you might need."

Dante looked up at me, his eyes begging me to get rid of her. I couldn't tell what he was thinking, but I knew I didn't want an audience for this. "I'm sure. Give us some time."

She nodded and headed back toward her office. Dante grabbed my hand and started to pull me in the opposite direction. We found ourselves in the precious metals part of the store. The ore was laid out in stacks. Dante released my hand and meandered around to the piles. His hand moved over one of the bars, thinking out loud. "No, I don't think silver."

My eyes moved to the armed guards that were patrolling around the perimeter of the store. "We're going to get caught."

"Then we spend a lot of money here." He moved to another stack, running a finger over another ingot. "Platinum perhaps, it does compliment my skin so beautifully."

That was the moment I knew exactly what he was doing. Falling to my knees, I looked up at him. "Gold has always been your color."

"Gold it is." He moved to the stack of ingots and perched on the edge. He placed a delicate hand beside him before smiling. "This was a good choice." I waited for him to say something, this was a game we hadn't played before. The pounding of my heart almost made me miss him snapping his fingers, followed by, "Well, get to it."

I crawled across the floor to him, coming up to my knees at his feet. He was wearing his favorite pair of leather boots, and I knew exactly what he wanted. I caught one of them in my hands, pressing my lips to the toe. I systematically worked my way up until I pressed a kiss to his thigh. I repeated the process with the other leg, a smirk crossing my face when he perfumed for me with my lips pressed to his skin. He spread his legs in a clear invitation. And I took it, pulling a blade from my pocket and slicing through the fabric until I could get to his cock.

"Don't be so impatient." His laugh turned into a moan as I swallowed his cock to the balls. He was leaking a steady stream of his delectable slick straight down my throat. My cock shot achingly hard as I flicked my tongue along his length. His head fell forward, eyes rolling back as he fisted my hair in his hand. His grip was steady as he pulled me off him and up, so I was looking him in the eyes. "I need you inside me right now."

Chapter 9

Dante

I was desperate for him, and I was tired of pretending I wasn't. His cock was hard in my hand as I moved it down to cup his knot through the pants. His hands came down to push them to the ground. I released my hold on his hair when he grabbed my hips to pull me down. He fell back to his knees, pushing my legs back until my knees rested against my chest. The lash of his tongue against my hole made me push back against him. He was taking too long.

"Alpha, I need it." His head popped up, surprise in his eyes.

"That sounded very unlike you, are you okay?"

My hand came down to caress his cheek, I loved how responsive he was. He noticed I was acting differently and immediately checked in. "I love you so much."

"I love you too, now tell me what's going on."

"Just exploring."

His head moved around as he mapped the guard's movements around the room. "Do you want to go home?"

"Not even a little bit."

His smirk was enough for me to fall in love with him all over. I was in his arms before I could process what was happening. His hardness pressing against my hole. I could feel his muscles moving as he lowered me down onto him. His cock stretched me right to the edge of pain before I finally relaxed around him. "I've missed you so much."

I came up to my knees, spinning around until I was looking at him. My moan echoed through the warehouse as I reached up to catch his face in my hands. "I've missed you more than you even know."

His hips started moving as he worked me until I collapsed against his chest. My hands tightened around his back as the orgasm took me. His knot starting to stretch me gave me the right amount of pain for my cock to explode, soaking the front of his shirt. That was all it took for him to slide the rest of the way inside me, the pressure making me orgasm around him. I felt myself tighten down around him, his cock still moving as he growled his pleasure into my ear. The moment he exploded inside me, the wall I built around the bond collapsed, letting me feel how desperate he was for me.

His hips kept moving, his growl vibrating across my throat as he pushed my head up. My hand came up to catch the back of his head, holding him close to me as he nipped at his mark. My cock throbbed between us, his cock throbbing inside me again. "My omega."

"You're in rut." It was the last thing I was able to say as he bit down, opening his mark again. The feeling of pleasure filling me as the bond flooded us with an even deeper connection. I was nearly boneless in his arms as he wrung every bit of pleasure out of me. It wasn't enough for him. Bradley's rut was intense and would go on for nearly as long as my heat would. The last thought I had before darkness claimed me was I wasn't sure how this was going to work when we got home.

I came to hours later, I knew I was home, but I wasn't sure how I had gotten there. Bradley's scent curled around me, centering me in a way that none of my other alphas could. So long as he was with me, I could handle anything. My men did different things for me, Richie was the passionate one, the one that gave me all the dark parts of himself. Evan was the peacemaker, and I loved him all the more for it. Xavier was my rock, there for me at every turn; he was my peace, my protector. Bradley was the quickest to calm me when my emotions ran too high. That was what he was doing for me right now, his arms tightening around me, making me relax for him.

"What time is it?" His voice vibrated against my back.

"If you would move I could see." I pushed against him. "You're heavy."

"Why would I when I have you right where I want you?"

I pushed against his chest as he rolled over on top of me. "Come on."

"Bradley, let him up." Xavier's voice made me turn my head to look at him. "He needs a shower before your rut starts up again."

I was relieved when the weight of my alpha moved from on top of me. Xavier was there to pull me from the bed, his arms tightening around me as he pulled me tight to his chest. I let him lead me out of the room. He pulled me into the bathroom, his hands on my waist were a welcomed center as he lifted me onto the vanity.

"Are you okay?" His question made me really think.

"I'm a little confused. How did we get home?"

"Siobhan called when Bradley went into rut. She closed down to let you finish, but when you both fell asleep she knew what it was."

"I owe her so much."

"You don't owe her anything. You cleaned out her supply of precious metals." Xavier's laugh made me look up at him confused. "She claimed it was impossible to get slick off metal. Tacked on a hefty cleaning fee too."

That was enough for me to relax and slide into the shower.

Chapter 10

Dante

I came out in front of the house as they finished unloading the ingots from the metal shop. I couldn't believe it had been less than a week since Bradley and I had our date, and I couldn't have been happier. Humming as I scanned the list, checking along as the delivery drivers unloaded the metal, there was much more than I expected there to be. I spent most of the morning directing the pack as they moved a colossal fortune in raw material. When I was finally able to sit down and decide what I was making, I drew a blank.

I had planned so many things, jewelry and decorative weapons were at the top of that list, but every time I started to reach for one of the designs, I hesitated. Nothing felt right. I flipped through them one last time, still not finding what I wanted. Backing out of the folder in my tablet, I started to exit the app, but hesitated when I saw the secret project folder. Opening it up, I flipped through them. They were all designs of things I planned to make for my pack. Now I didn't know if that was ever going to happen.

Looking at the designs brought too many painful memories to the surface. That was when I came upon the one I wanted to make for Xavier. It was perfect. Getting up, I stopped in the office to print out the pattern and headed to my smithy. There was a stack of ingots in the corner, and my forge was already hot and ready to go. One of the men had lit it for me hours ago judging by the amount of ash and coals in the hearth. I reached over and pulled one of the crucibles out and buried it in the heat. Spinning in place, I moved around my space, thinking about the things necessary to truly create what I planned. I dropped one of the gold ingots into the crucible, cutting it with just enough silver to assure the hardness of the final product. While it melted, I mentally ran through what I had been told.

I had come across it when I was doing a genealogical study on my pack. A blade and the story attached to it. A story that belonged to one of Xavier's ancestors. The blade had been lost to history, but the story survived. His mother told it best; an early ancestor of his was one of the first of humanity that presented in a way that was undeniable. One of the first omegas, marking the beginning of a new era for humanity. There were those that wanted to experiment on him, leaving him with no choice but to go into hiding. That part of the story always made my heart ache. I couldn't even begin to imagine the fear he must have felt. He managed to keep his family hidden and protected for decades before the other royals found them. He survived, thrived even, and created Omega Services to protect people like him. And all the while, the only thing he carried with him was a gold dagger, a rather ornate one at that. One that I intended to recreate as a gift to my alpha.

Before I could think too hard, the steam whistle went off, telling me the metal was ready. I pulled on gloves and the apron before reaching for the tongs and pulling the crucible out. Stirring the metal with a steel rod, I moved across the room as quickly as I could, tipping it over so the metal filled the dagger blank I had. Flames danced around the top of the blank as I set the crucible back into the forge. It took a little bit of time for it to cool, allowing me to go to my jewel collection so I could select the right ones. I had so many to choose from and I couldn't quite figure out which ones would look the best. I finally gave in and consulted the description of the blade I had found. I sighed, realizing that it was a bit more complicated than I cared to admit. I ended up with a medium sized tanzanite for the handle and a handful of sapphire chips to decorate the rest of it.

By the time I returned, Xavier was in the forge waiting for me. He was standing beside the table, studying the blade as it was cooling. "Hi, alpha."

"Dante." He beamed when he saw me, his eyes lighting up like I was his everything. It hit me again in that moment how lucky I was to have him. "What are you making?"

"It's a surprise."

"For me?"

I nodded. "And you can't ruin it, so go sit down and let me work."

He huffed but did as I asked, taking a seat in the corner of the room. Going back to the piece, I smiled when I realized it was nearly cool enough to etch. Turning on my hose, I took some time to quench the piece, the steam coming off it made a satisfying sound. When I was sure it was cooled, I wrapped my gloved hand around the handle. Rushing over to the water jug, I buried the blade inside and held it there until the water stopped boiling. I was in the zone, completely focused on what I was doing. Setting the blade in the clamp, I started my work by opening up the end of the handle until there was a large enough space to mount the tanzanite. From there, I worked on the intricate spirals that would grace the handle. Time slipped by as I worked my way down the piece, adding touches here and there. By the time I finished carving the mounts for the gems, my back was screaming at me from bending over. I was nearly done, carefully placing the gems one at a time until I was satisfied. Standing up, I released the blade from the clamps before taking it to Xavier. "What did you make me, sweet omega?" His words were enough to make my heart flutter in my chest.

"I might have done some secret research."

"Why am I not surprised?"

My foot tapped as my nerves started to rise. "I thought you might like this." I handed it to him. "I know the original is lost, but I managed to track down some notes about it."

His eyes moved down as he studied the blade, he was silent for a moment too long, I hoped I hadn't miscalculated. "Baby, I don't know..."

"I can always make you something else."

"No." He reached out, cupping my cheek in his hand. "I love it."

Chapter 11

Xavier

I couldn't take watching Dante suffer any longer, it made my heart ache. Ever since Dante had recreated that blade for me, I had felt like a failure. He saw me as his protector, the only one that would never leave him. And I was failing in that first one, it couldn't stand. Nothing about this was normal and I needed to fix it pronto, just like I had all those years ago when Penelope left.

Watching Evan coming out of the nest, I considered going in there and checking on Dante. The pain of Penelope's rejection had hit him harder than I expected, and he hadn't gotten out of bed in two weeks. I stopped the beta as he moved past me with a mostly full plate. "He's still not eating?"

"He's barely moving." The concern was clear on Evan's face as he spoke. "I don't know how much longer we can let this go on without doing something."

"I'm aware. Let me handle this."

"Take care of our omega." He placed a hand on my shirt as he continued, "Whatever it takes."

"What do you mean by that?"

He patted my shoulder as he moved past me. "You'll understand when you get in there."

That was all it took for me to push into the room. His scent was the first thing that hit me, the acrid smell of sorrow mixed with his own delicious one. Every part of me screamed that he needed me. It hadn't been this bad this morning when I went to class.

No, this wouldn't do.

Crossing the room, I slid into the bed beside him, reaching out and pulling him into my arms. He tensed for a moment before relaxing there, his arms tightening around me weakly. He was much too small, feeling fragile in my arms. I could feel his ribs pushing against his skin, the beating of his heart behind what weeks before had been hard muscle. I searched for what I needed to do to reach him.

"Why'd she have to leave me?" He sounded broken, his voice weak.

"I don't know."

"It hurts so bad."

My heart ached hearing how much pain he was in. "I know it does." The vibrating of my phone in my pocket made me hesitate, but I ignored it, focused on the omega in my arms. "When was the last time you ate anything?"

"I'm not hungry."

"You barely touched your dinner." The next words out of my mouth were cut off by Evan coming back into the room.

He held a phone in his hand, I could hear a woman's voice on the other end cussing up a storm. "It's Calliope."

"I don't want to talk to her right now," Dante whispered.

I took the phone from the beta, pressing it to my ear in time to hear Calliope asking, "Did he seriously hang up on me?"

"Calliope," I sighed. I really didn't have time for this. "I'm kind of dealing with something right now."

"So, dealing with the dying omega takes a backseat to whatever you're doing. Okay, got it." If only she knew.

Dante tapped on my chest, I put it on speaker so he could reply to her. "I'm right here."

"Dante." She sounded relieved to hear his voice. "You don't sound good."

"He's not." I cut in before he could deny it. "Penelope leaving really did a number on him."

"Fucking alphas don't remember a damn thing, I swear." I could feel the rage in her words. "Why do they even bother making everyone take biology if no one pays attention?"

"You're not making any sense."

She swore a few more times before coming back on. "If you had paid attention, you would remember that rejection is deadly to omegas. Especially a rejection that cut as deeply as this one has."

"What else did we forget?"

"How quickly you should have reacted, for one," she snapped. "But let's forget about that for the time being. There's only one solution now."

"Which is?"

"Someone needs to claim him." She sighed. "The bond will keep him more regulated while he deals with it."

"Are you okay with that, baby boy?" I pressed a gentle kiss to his forehead.

"I guess," he whispered.

I hung up, handing the phone to Evan. I wasn't willing to give my omega a single second to rethink this. I couldn't lose him. He didn't fight me as I stripped him slowly, his body much smaller than it should be. A sense of urgency slammed into me, making me release him and strip myself. My cock reacted to his scent thickening, taking that worry from my mind with it. I was so over my head, I was working on instinct here. My hand slid between his legs, catching his cock and the slick that was slowly leaking from it. Hormones were a hell of a thing, making our bodies react when our hearts weren't into it. His legs came back, hitting his chest, I slid between them, reaching over to grab the lube from the table.

"I know we're skipping a lot of the foreplay, but we can't miss this part." He offered me a weak smile as I opened the bottle, covering a few fingers before sliding them inside him.

He reacted to that by letting out a weak moan as I worked my fingers along his prostate, milking it until he was wet for me. Pulling my fingers out, I pushed into him as quickly as I could, sure that I was racing against a clock I didn't even know existed. He was fading, I was sure of it. I worked him until he opened enough for me to knot him, his eyes closing as his head tilted. His body reacting when he didn't know how. My head snapped forward before he could deny it. As I caught his skin there between my teeth, I lathered the spot I had chosen with my tongue before biting down. The explosion of his blood on my tongue relieved an ache in my chest I hadn't acknowledged until that moment. It took no time before the bond exploded between us and I was flooded with just how deep his sorrow ran.

It was overwhelming, making me crumble. Pulling him with me so we were both lying on our sides, his head came to rest on my shoulder, as his eyes closed. I couldn't stand the thought that I had almost lost him. As much as I wanted to hate Penelope, I hated to admit she likely did the right thing. Two omegas rarely worked together, regardless of the circumstances that the pack came together. His breathing evened out as he slid into what would hopefully be a restful sleep. As I looked down at him, I promised myself he would never have to go through this again.

I knew exactly what I needed to do. Three phone calls and two days later me and Dante were pulling into the parking lot for the renaissance faire. This wasn't a place where either of us went on a regular basis, but I had made sure Dante would be safe here. I got out as soon as I parked, coming around to open his door for him. He took the arm I offered him. "Why are we here?"

"You'll see." I smiled down at him for a moment, leading him through the gathered crowds to the back of the fairgrounds.

There was a nearly abandoned area that was set up for a display that hadn't opened yet. That was the precise reason I had brought Dante here. We moved past the ropes as I led him beneath the stage. The space opened up to reveal a large smithy, and I relished watching Dante's eyes widen with happiness. At the other end of the room was the blacksmith, someone that my omega knew well.

"Eddy," I called out, making Dante take a breath.

The beta turned around, his deeply tanned skin and overly wrinkled face was open, and a warm smile was cresting there. "Dante, it's been years."

"It has." My omega offered the older man his hand. "What do I owe the pleasure?"

"Your alpha didn't tell you?" The beta flashed his eyes to me, when I shook my head he stammered, "I thought we could work on a piece together for the charity auction."

The way Dante lit up warmed my heart. "Let's go."

Two hours later I was standing on the stage, waiting for the moment to begin the auction. I wasn't entirely sure what they planned on creating, but I couldn't wait to see. The podium I was standing in front of had a pair of screens embedded in the wood, allowing me to watch what was happening beneath the stage. Sparks flew as they took hammers to hard metal, working the piece until it was smooth. A small crowd had gathered to watch the process; I could hear them murmuring as time passed. But I wasn't worried about them, I was more fascinated by the way my omega moved. His muscles flexing as he raised the hammer for his blow, I could almost hear the sizzle of his sweat hitting the hot metal when he pulled back to avoid the sparks he had created.

There was something mesmerizing about the way he worked, each movement perfectly timed and executed to achieve his aim, the sword starting to take shape. It was another classical design, one that most people could get anywhere. What made it unique was Eddy, Edmundo Garcia, world renowned bladesmith. To have one of his weapons was a treasured thing for most. That was sure to drive up the price. My eyes moved from the screen, scanning the crowd that had collected in front of me. I doubted many of them had the money this sword would bring, they weren't who I was looking for anyway. I spotted her hiding in the shadows in the very back.

She looked older than I remembered her, her curls falling around her head in loose spirals. When she turned to catch my eye, I was certain it was Amani. She was supposed to run as far as she could, get away from everything that came with being royal, it had been eating her alive for as long as I could remember. I had never been more relieved than when she left. She should have a say in her life and not be forced into some box our parents wanted her in. I started to move, started to go to her when the timer on my watch beeped, making me look away for a split second. When I looked back, she was gone. I struggled to push the image of her away for now, hoping that she ran as far from Raleigh as she could.

Reaching for the microphone, I forced a smile as I brought it to my lips. "Welcome, all, to today's auction." There was a roar as the crowd exploded around me. "Our guests this afternoon have been working most of the day to create something truly special for our winner." I cut to the close-up of the sketches they were working off of. "Now, as we can see, they are working on making a Spartan sword." I reached down to change the camera again in time to catch Dante lifting the blade into the air. The metal was still glowing, making my omega look very much like a god of the forge. He spun in place, shoving the metal into a barrel of oil, making flames jump along the surface. The oil clung to the blade as he retrieved it, making flames dance along its length as he turned and dropped the blade into a barrel of water. I smiled, cutting the camera to where Eddy was preparing to etch the blade. "Now they're nearly done. Let's start the bidding...say... two fifty?"

The bids flew by, there was nothing more thrilling than the moment the stage opened, the mechanism bringing Dante and Eddy up as they finished the work they were doing. The blade gleamed in the light as they moved. The flurry of bids was making my head spin as I fought to keep up with them, closing them when I heard a truly astounding amount. Dante joined me as we took the transfer. I loved feeling my omega's contentment, his scent clung to me as it always did after he spent hours in his shop. I couldn't get enough of it.

His head turned, his words making me feel like he was reading my mind. "Take me home, I need you."

Chapter 12

Penelope

I needed to do something, not being able to find the matchmaker was driving me crazy. There were only so many places a dirty matchmaker could be. I had long ago claimed a spot in the parking lot across from Omega Services. The evening had been spent searching the lot for his car. My fingers tapped a rhythm on the steering wheel as I waited. There wasn't much else I could do. God knows I didn't want to go home; I couldn't take Dante's sneering at me. Pain seized my heart as I remembered the last day we were truly happy.

"I get my designation test today." Dante sounded excited, and I loved that for him.

He pulled me into his arms, pressing a kiss to my lips. "Mine is tomorrow."

"Are you nervous?"

"No." He was so sure of himself, I wished I could be so certain. When Calliope, his twin, got her results yesterday she came back as an omega. One of the first things we are taught in school is when twins do happen, which isn't often, they never have different designations. "I can't wait to be your beta."

My next words were cut off by my phone ringing, it was a number I didn't recognize. Putting it to my ear, I was graced by a masculine voice. "Is this Penelope?"

"It is." I slid from Dante's arms, pressing a kiss to his forehead before pulling away so I could have a more private conversation. "What can I help you with?"

"I'm calling from Omega Services."

"My designation test isn't until tomorrow."

I could hear him typing as he spoke. "I'm aware of that. It's just procedure that we make this call."

"Something tells me you don't call everyone who gets tested."

"You would be right there." He seemed to be trying to put me at ease . "We call people who have a high likelihood of coming back as omegas, we like to check in and see if there is a potential pack in the works, help get suppressants if necessary, just standard things."

"You're not going to offer me suppressants, are you?"

"No, I am the matchmaker assigned to you. I was calling to see if you had a pack in mind?"

I chewed on my bottom lip for a moment before starting. "I do."

"Awesome. If you can give me their names?"

I proceeded to rattle off everyone's names, hesitating a moment before adding, "Dante Allister."

"Having two omegas in the same pack is unusual, but not unheard of. There is one thing you should be made aware of... A potential conflict."

"Tell me." It was an order, one that he followed. When he was done, my pulse was racing, I knew I needed to leave, knew I couldn't stay there in a pack with that alpha. I had to get away. "Can you arrange for someone to come and get me from Dante's house?"

"I'll have someone there in ten minutes."

I didn't take any time to think about what I was doing, I couldn't. Panic seized in my chest as my heart threatened to pound out of it. I couldn't stay here, it was too close to home. Leaving was my only option. Running back into the bedroom, I grabbed a backpack out of the closet and started tossing clothes into it. Reaching down, my hand closed around Dante's hoodie, I wanted to take it with me. My brain caught up in that moment, I couldn't leave him. I loved him more than anything. We could make it work. Shaking my head, I pushed that idea away, shoving the hoodie into the bag beside my clothes. It was the only part of this pack I allowed myself.

I was heading toward the front door as Dante called out to me, "Penelope, where are you going in such a hurry?"

"I'm sorry." My hand closed around the knob, it almost twisted in my hand as I heard someone coming up beside me. I couldn't look, but his scent gave him away. "Take care of him, Xavier. I need you to promise me."

"You don't have to do this. We can fix anything."

"You can't fix this."

"Let us try," Xavier pleaded

I chanced a look at him, his concern was plain for anyone to see. "No one can fix this. Take care of Dante."

I opened the door and rushed out before either of them could stop me.

The door opening made me jump, my head turning as I watched Rhys slip into the passenger seat. "What the fuck do you want?"

"You know, if you're stalking someone it works best to pay attention."

"Why are you here?" I should be doing anything but pushing back against him. I knew this man was a killer, knew what he was capable of.

"I couldn't keep you off my mind." He reached over and caught my chin, applying just enough pressure that I couldn't pull away from him. "You have crawled under my skin, and now you will never be rid of me."

I slapped his hand away, reaching for the door handle with the other. Catching it, I froze when Rhys put his hand on my shoulder. "Let go of me."

"I'm not going anywhere, so you should get really comfortable with me being around."

I huffed, crossing my arms over my chest. "My pack won't allow this."

"You don't have a pack." His laugh just pissed me off. "And I highly doubt that Dante or his pack would care if you disappeared."

I wish I could refute that statement, but I wasn't entirely sure he was wrong. "Fuck all the way off."

"I won't ever 'fuck all the way off'— as you so eloquently put it." He invaded my space, his head filling the spot left when my head turned. I flinched at the thought, but I refused to show him I was scared. "I intend to crawl as deeply under your skin as you have crawled under mine, and there is nothing you can do to stop me."

"You can't come in and declare that I'm yours."

"I think I just did." He nipped at a spot on my neck, making me shiver for him. "And I'm sure you'll find that your body agrees with me."

"It doesn't work that way."

He lapped along that spot, the feeling made my toes curl, my perfume filled the car until we were drowning in it. "I think you'll find it does." We sat in silence for a long moment before he spoke again. "So, who are we stalking?"

I refused to dignify that with a response.

"You can either tell me or I can get it out of you." His hands moved across my body, tweaking one of my nipples. The sharp pain forced me to bite my lip to fight a moan. "And I'm very good at getting information out of people."

"Fine," I sighed. "But we're doing this my way."

I threw the car into drive and peeled out of the parking lot, aiming the car toward the highway. We rode in silence for a while until I pulled off into an opening in the trees. Putting it in park, all we could hear were the clicks as the car cooled.

"It all started with the call to that fucking matchmaker." I sighed. "It was all bad luck that kicked it off. The process is pretty simple, you go to the office and get handed a folder filled with profiles of packs. But I already had my pack. At least I thought I did."

"What happened?"

"We went through all the motions." I could see the desk and the folder in front of me. "None of the packs worked for me. So, I went home, well, what home was at that point. The house that Dante and I shared with his pack. Two days later, the matchmaker called me, asking if I'd made my choice."

"That was when you found out about my connection to Richie."

"It was. I had a panic moment realizing who he was. That he wasn't who I thought he was." A thought occurred to me, and I couldn't let the opportunity pass. "Why did you kill my mother?"

"We aren't talking about me right now."

I shook my head. "If you want me to trust you I need to know."

"Fine." His growl made me want to shrink into my seat. "You want to know why? I'll fucking tell you why. Your bitch of a mother beat the fuck out of your older brother."

"I don't have a brother. Other than Cain."

"You're right. You don't have another one anymore." I couldn't tell if he was lying to me or not. "I found her after she beat your brother to death. She wasn't even arrested. Cops get away with absolutely everything. They came to the house and took him out on a stretcher. I didn't know a nine-year-old could be so small." He looked truly haunted as he talked about this, he wasn't detached at all; nothing like the heartless serial killer he was. It was...so...human. "I broke into the coroner's office, stole her records, read about every vicious thing she did to him, and then I recreated them on her body, as best as I could."

"What about her pack? They didn't try to stop you?"

"They tried." He nodded.

"But they were unsuccessful?"

"Obviously." His voice dropped a few octaves, "Normally, I would have at least threatened the baby. There was always a baby."

"Me."

He nodded. "I guess it was."

"You don't even know the names of the children, the innocent babies whose lives you have tied to your crimes, do you?"

"I know the name of every single child that my crimes have touched." He held his hand up. "My first was a boy, his name was Christian Solo, his mother starved his older sister. Said she had to be the," he held his fingers up and made quotes in the air, "'perfect, tiny omega.' The boy turned out to be the omega, has a pack that loves and protects him like he is their world."

"Jesus."

"The second was a girl, Nicole Masters, she grew up to be a beta, married another beta, and they have several children. Her father neglected her older brother so badly he ate anything he could get his hands on. Until he managed to get his hands on his father's illegally obtained pistol."

"Enough."

"You're curious why I don't know a thing about you? Why you were the one I didn't keep tabs on?" he pressed.

"I think I need to know."

"The things they were doing to you, an child barely two years old, made me see red." His hands shook as he spoke. "I lost it, tore the whole pack apart and called in a favor."

"What favor?"

"I don't know if I can tell you that."

I huffed, not even trying to keep the annoyance out of my voice. "You want me to trust you, but I need you to be honest with me for that to work."

"Fine, I called in a favor from someone who owed me at the Marshall's Service. It was my one and only favor, and he agreed to it under the condition that I never try to find out anything about you."

"You left every other child with their parents. You only ever killed one of them. Why did you take me?"

"Because there was no one left to take care of you. I had no choice. I certainly wasn't leaving a fucking child alone in that slaughterhouse."

"What made you break your pattern?"

His growl made me flinch. "Enough questions."

He got out of the car, slamming the door behind him. That reaction told me I had hit a nerve. Something had made him break his pattern, but I wasn't sure if I even wanted to know what it was.

I didn't even remember my parents or their pack. I'd been told about them, of course. Had seen a few of the news articles, but that was a poor substitute for actually knowing them. The pack that raised me had treated me like I was their princess, making sure I had everything I needed. And they succeeded at that, I never wanted for a thing.

Chapter 13

Rhys

I couldn't tell Penelope the things I had witnessed the night I killed her mother. It had taken me years to come to terms with it. And she hadn't known I killed her parent's entire pack that night until I told her two days ago. How that was even possible, I didn't know. But I knew what happened that night, it was seared into my memory.

I came upon the house late at night, there shouldn't be anyone awake, not that it would matter. I was here to do a job and I wasn't leaving until it was done. I just needed to find my way in, it should be simple enough. This pack had multiple children, but something about the looming house made me suspicious. It was too quiet, too well kept considering the neighborhood around it wasn't uniform at all. The beige color it was painted made it stand out among the blues and greens. As I came around the back of the house, my heart started to beat harder in my chest. This wasn't going to be like my normal kills. Going after a detective wasn't the best idea I'd ever had, but I couldn't let what she had done to her child stand. The FBI had a term for what I was.

Injustice Collector

I smiled when I thought about that, it fit me like a well-worn leather glove. And I was here to collect on one more injustice. She may have been above the law, but she wasn't above bleeding out beneath my blade. I would make her pack watch. Passing by one of the windows, I peeked in, a wicked grin crossing my face when I spotted an empty room. It was shrouded in darkness, but I could tell there was no one inside. Pulling on my gloves, I removed the screen and tested the window, surprised to find it unlocked. As I climbed into the room, I scanned around me trying to figure out where I was in the house.

I had just cleared the window and closed it behind me when I heard the knob turning. Running to the open closet, I hid inside, leaving the door open just enough for me to see what was happening in the room beyond it. They came in and flicked on the light, my eyes adjusted quickly, letting me see a woman wearing a police uniform. My smile twisted into more of a smirk as I realized she was my chosen victim. She hadn't noticed me yet, it was the perfect opportunity to strike, but something told me to wait. Putting her back to me, she moved a mouse on a desk across the room making the monitor come to life. When she stood up I got a glimpse of what was on the screen.

Children, and young ones at that, performing acts that no child should know exists. It was vile, making my stomach roll and rage start to build inside me. My hand shook as I reached for the door, not even fighting the urge to burst from the closet. I was close to launching myself at her when a small man came into the room. He went to her, laying his head against her shoulder as they watched the screen together. It was then that I realized how badly I had miscalculated this. I wasn't leaving. There wasn't a chance in hell I was leaving these people with a child. My strategy changed in moments as I planned out the kills. Bursting from the closet with my blade in my hand, they spun to watch me. The panic on their faces was a good start. I charged them, getting between them before they had time to react. I caught the alpha's throat with the blade, taking out the threat allowed me to focus on her omega.

I didn't take time to watch the blood hit the floor before I had the omega by the hair. "Tell me where the rest of your pack is."

"Not on your fucking life." He was entirely too calm for having just lost one of his alphas.

"Guess she wasn't your favorite." I shrugged. "But I bet I can get them to come running if I start torturing you."

"You wouldn't dare."

I moved to the desk, dragging the omega behind me. Adjusting my grip, I slammed him face first into the monitor. "Sure seems like I just did." I repeated the motion, his pathetic attempts to hit me as I tightened my grip on his hair almost made me laugh.

A twisted grin spread across my face when I heard the footsteps coming. Lifting him so he was in front of me, I held the blade at my side as I waited. They came through the door at the same time, filling the room as they fanned out. I couldn't stop the smirk when I saw the panic in their eyes. "Let my omega go."

"You must be his favorite."

"I'm his alpha. Release him now." He was so full of bravado.

Opening the omega's throat, I dropped his bleeding body as I moved to meet the charging alpha head on. His fists were flying, little good it would do him. I ducked under one of his punches and slammed the blade home between his ribs. Twisting the knife, I punctured his lung. Ripping it from his side, I caught the beta that was flying at me on my right. Twisting, I tossed him into one of the other men. They fell to the ground and I caught the last alpha as he approached me.

He had a blade in his hand and was watching me, the way I moved. It was cute that he thought he was better than me. I was twenty-five, an alpha in my prime, he was nearing fifty. I backed up until I was standing above the two on the ground. My arm came down, slamming the blade handle deep into the beta's skull. I kicked the body back and killed the alpha the same way. My head came up as the last alpha started to move. He was slow, taking measured steps. He telegraphed his strike, letting me catch his hand in the air and slam the blade through his heart.

A wave of satisfaction ripped through me as I watched their blood soak into the carpet. The crying of a child pulled my attention to the hallway. I turned, heading toward the wailing before looking down at my hands. They were soaked through with the blood of her parents; I couldn't be near the child like this. Heading to the bathroom, I ran my hands under the warm water, putting soap on them. I enjoyed watching the bubbles turn pink. Another insistent wail snapped me out of the moment.

Pain ripped through my chest at the memory of what I had found in that room. Penelope was there, surrounded by toys and dolls. Things that a child should have, but it was the same room from those vile pictures.

"What are you thinkin' about?" Liam's voice broke through the fog of thought.

I offered him a weak smile. "The past."

"I try not to dwell on that." The omega took a seat beside me.

"Kind of hard not to when the past smacks you in the face."

"Want to talk about it?"

"Not really," I sighed. "But I probably should."

"Tell me all about it."

"I slaughtered her parent's whole pack." His nod was not the answer I expected. "And when they were dead I called in a favor to keep her protected."

"That must have been one hell of a thing you did to earn such a large favor."

"It was." I nodded. "And I called it back in spades."

"What made this one different?"

"Her mother was a cop."

He smirked. "That's reason enough to kill her, but why the rest of the pack? Why the omega?"

"They were making and selling illicit images of children, their own children." There were only so many ways I could dance around this.

"You don't have to explain." The omega put a hand on my knee. "I get it."

"I can't stand people who do that to children. I just lost it. I couldn't leave her there like that. I wouldn't have been able to forgive myself."

"And you couldn't call the cops."

I nodded. "I couldn't risk anyone getting their hands on her."

"And now you're obsessed."

"I wouldn't say obsessed." He shot me a dirty look. "Okay, I'm obsessed. She's just so breathtaking. Everything about her makes my heart sing. She is mine, no questions."

"And I thought my situation was complicated."

"You have a whole pack waiting for you." I couldn't stop the curiosity. "Why haven't you gone home?"

"I don't have one." He stood, crossing the room to grab his pack of blunts. Handing me one of them, he kept the other and we lit them in tandem. "I honestly don't know what I'm going to do."

"We have nothing but time."

"I was in an accelerated program at Omega Services to work in their police department." He had that faraway look that I saw in the mirror as he spoke. It made me wonder who it was that was responsible for that. "I was supposed to start my undercover assignment the week after my heat. I was supposed to get sold into the trafficking network and bring it all down."

"Who came up with that stupid fucking idea?"

"I don't even remember anymore." He took a long drag from the blunt. "But the plan changed last minute. Almost as soon as I went into heat, me and my alpha, Flynn, were called into headquarters. We were told there was an informant for the group we were targeting that was in the planning of this, they suspected it was one of my pack."

"Who were they sending you after?"

"The Irish Mob."

I let it go. "That pack of yours, are they all cops?"

"Fuck no." His denial was so quick I couldn't help but laugh. "I didn't even want to be one."

"What changed?"

"They offered to buy me a house. To set me up for life. My family was one of the poorest in the town I grew up in." I understood that desperation. "My pack is all around my age. I don't know what they ended up doing."

"So, you had to go under earlier than planned?"

"Flynn was pissed, he hated the idea to begin with. Then, our boss dropped the worst of it. Flynn was the only one allowed to mark me." My heart ached as I watched him reach up and rub a spot near his heart. I couldn't imagine what it would be like for either of them to be separated as they were. "So, my heat came and went. My pack fell asleep around me, and Flynn took me."

"You said they lost you. How?"

"I had a tracker implanted, the man who bought me cut it out." He showed me the scar on his arm. "They had no way of knowing where I was."

"And this man?"

"My first victim." There was a viciousness in his eyes that warmed my heart.

His eyes filled with sadness, he needed comfort, but I wasn't the one to give it to him. There wasn't much that I could do. Tracking Flynn down was at the very top of my list. If he was anything like me, I knew he would ache to comfort his omega. If not, I would happily watch him bleed. I couldn't stay around here, I needed to go, I needed to hunt. To kill, to make someone bleed, but I hesitated to leave Liam alone.

"Go." His words were filled with something close to resentment, but as I turned to look at him, tears were starting to form there. "I'll be fine."

Deciding it was best to leave the omega to his moment, I left, closing the door behind me. Heading to the car, I could feel the hair on the back of my neck standing up. There was someone watching me, and I needed to know who it was. A smile crossed my face as I headed back toward the front door. A rustling to the right made me hesitate, deciding to try and come up behind whoever it was. I went left, aiming for the wood pile on that side of the house. Circling around the building, I came up around the other side.

Now that I was close enough I could see it was a man standing there. He wasn't much shorter than I was and was, watching through bushes, waiting for something. The wind was blowing toward me, allowing me to catch his scent. This alpha was watching the house, the house that I had just left an omega alone inside of. Making a split-second decision, I gripped the handle of my knife and closed in on him.

My hand closed around his hair, pulling his head back as I leveled the blade to his throat. "You'd better have a good explanation as to why you're sneaking around in the middle of the night."

"Is Liam in there?"

"I don't know who that is."

"Three people escaped that prison." He was so confident. "Landon Costa, you, and my omega. I didn't find him with Landon, so I assumed you'd have him here with you."

"So, what if I do?"

There was relief in his voice when he spoke again, "Tell me he's okay."

"Why would I tell you anything after you sold him?"

There was so much rage in my voice, I longed to open his throat with that blade. But I hesitated for a moment, this had to be Flynn. He used my moment of hesitation to his advantage, slamming his head back, so he pulled out of my grasp. He ducked under the blade, spinning as he caught my wrist in his hand. The pressure was enough to make me drop the blade. I managed to catch it with my free hand before he could, my eyes coming up to catch his. His hands were in the air as he backed away from me. "It's not like that. I've been looking for him for seven years now."

"You'd better start talking." There was no room for argument. He spent the next twenty minutes filling me in on what happened from his end. Anger rose inside me as I listened to every word that came out of his mouth. The desperation was almost palpable. When he was finished I nodded, that story hadn't been easy for him to tell. I turned my back to him, heading to my car. Getting to the driver's door, I called out to him before I climbed inside. "He's in the cabin. If you hurt him you won't make it to sunrise."

Chapter 14

Dante

Penelope was pacing the living room, giving me the ability to study the beautiful woman she had become. She was tall for an omega, with curly black hair and vibrant blue eyes. Her curves were distracting as all hell, making it nearly impossible to focus on what she was actually saying. Penelope was in pain, or annoyed, I couldn't tell which from her tone. I could tell how attentive my mates were to her, and all that did was just piss me off. She had run from us, abandoning me when I needed her the most. It took everything in me to focus on the present and not get lost in those painful memories, but try as I might, I failed.

I couldn't understand what I had done so wrong that Penelope had to leave. We weren't perfect, far from it, but no human is. I can't remember the last time we disagreed about anything more intense than what to make for dinner. There was no reason for it. She just hadn't wanted me, hadn't wanted my pack. And it was my fault. It had to be. Why my test had to come back with me as an omega was beyond me. She should have been our omega, the center of our pack. I couldn't help but feel like biology had given me the short end of the stick, and I was stuck trying to be something I clearly wasn't meant to be.

What kind of omega didn't even have the energy to get out of bed and check on his pack?

Me, that was who. Even though the idea of moving was too much, I couldn't even remember the last time I ate. My stomach growling told me it had been too long, but I just couldn't force myself to eat, especially when nothing smelled good to me anymore. It felt like a piece of me had been torn out, and all I was left with was a gaping wound. The pain wasn't physical, but it might as well have been.

"You have to eat something." I had just enough energy to turn and look at Bradley where he stood at the door, plate in hand. "You haven't eaten in three days."

"What's the point?"

My voice was so weak, I was surprised when he heard me. "The point is your pack loves you, and we're all going to be really fucking pissed if you die."

"You all wanted Penelope as your omega anyway."

"Is that what you think?" He crossed the room, setting the plate on the nightstand before sitting beside me. His hand fell on my thigh, his thumb rubbing in small circles. He only did that when he was scared or nervous. "It's not the truth. We knew a long time ago you were probably our omega. It was kind of hard to miss. We all thought Penelope was going to be a beta."

"Then why did she leave?"

"I don't have that answer for you."

"I had to have done something."

He reached over and took my chin between his fingers before bringing my head up so I was looking at him. "You are the sweetest, most loving person I have ever met. There isn't a mean bone in your whole body. It wasn't your fault she left. She told us to apologize to you. Does that seriously sound like it's your fault?"

Growing up with Penelope should have been enough to quell the instinctive omega jealousy, but I found myself increasingly irritated at her very existence. Her being here put pressure on me and my pack. A point that was underscored by the way Xavier was stalking across the room like he wanted to tear someone apart.

My head fell back to the tablet that sat in front of me on the table. There were a few last-minute adjustments that I needed to make to the design of the blade before it was ready for casting. This particular weapon was for ritualistic purposes, or at least that was what the person who had commissioned it through my legal business said. Flipping to a new page, I started the sketch. I had a certain client that was particular in what they used for their less than legal purposes. I knew as much considering the last three blades I had made for them were currently sitting in the police evidence locker. Each weapon they ordered was unique in ways that made me wonder exactly how their mind worked. I had been trying to work this design out for the last two weeks and the deadline was coming up, and it was coming quickly.

This shouldn't have been a difficult process, they always asked for some variation of the same weapon. Axes, all of them. The handles were getting shorter with each one they had me make. It was almost like they were getting more confident over time. I was glad for that, it gave me the opportunity to push my skill at metalwork to a higher level. Each piece I created was more lethal than the last, as per their specifications. This was the thing I loved doing the most, and every piece I put out was deadly in its beauty.

My pack was arguing around me, debating what they were going to do to better protect the other omega. I hated that; it made me uncomfortable to even think of one of my men caring about her so deeply. Especially when she had abandoned our pack because she couldn't share. Running from me after rallying the entire pack around her, after courting these men, and having them make her the center of their world. Truthfully, she had been the center of mine for much longer. Our connection had always felt somehow more significant than the ones we had with our pack. That had made her rejection hurt all the worse. She was the glue that held us together, nearly none of the men were interested in me.

Or they hadn't been at the time.

Except for Xavier, he was always my rock. He was always there when I needed him. But the omegas were the attraction of our little group. Penelope, Amani, me, and my twin. At least everyone thought Amani was going to be an omega, much like they thought I was going to be a beta. But mostly the girls, alphas were never really interested in me. Not even when it became obvious I was an omega. All except Xavier. It always felt like I was the only one he wanted, and so far, he had proven that as fact. I loved him all the more for it. He had no qualms about telling anyone who would listen just that. My twin was lucky, her pack found her when she needed them most. I wasn't as fortunate. My heart hurt at the thought that I might be losing the men I loved to the woman who left us. Now she was back and fitting right in like she had never left. My men seemed to have picked up where they left off with her.

Once again, I was left out in the dark with the people I loved. Rage guided my hand as I sketched. The lines of the axe were angry, swirling things that would make for some vicious nightmares. I could already see the way I would lay and sculpt the metal. Titanium turned the prettiest colors when you treated it right. The handle of this one was short, the curve of the blade coming down in sort of a guard, this would be good for close quarters combat. I was truly in love with this design. When I finished, I realized the room around me was empty.

I set the tablet down and headed to bed. Coming up to the nest, I could already smell Penelope's white chocolate scent mixing with the woodsy scents of my alphas. I couldn't bring myself to go inside, instead, turning around and heading toward my smithy. Grabbing my tablet on the way through the living room, I stopped by the office and printed the guide for the weapon. The sound of the printer whirring was enough for me to forget that my problems existed. There was nothing I could do about it but let things take their course. Taking the sheets, I moved into the smithy to my worktable. Setting the blueprint out on the table, I really studied it for a moment.

Knowing it was easier to start with a single solid center, I turned on the furnace and waited while it heated up. Making sure the two crucibles I would need were in the flames, I took a seat close to the fire. Sitting there, my mind started to wander. Everything was set up to have my ideal pack, with my dream girl beside me. We had all grown up together. My twin was even mated to her brother. Everything was laid out for us, all we had to do was take it. Not that she wanted to. No, when it came right down to our first heat she ran to Omega Services. Left me alone, not only to deal with my own emotions, but so many volatile alphas that just watched the woman they loved run from them. And I couldn't help but feel like the consolation prize. I don't know precisely what spurred her decision to leave us, but even if I did, it wouldn't have hurt any less.

I was just about to lose myself in the metal when a sound from behind me made me look up. Watching Xavier come at me was like watching shadows move. His skin was deep onyx, the forge making his skin seem to shimmer from its purple undertones. His locs were up, held tight to his head by a clip, but I knew when they were down they danced above his shoulders. "Hey, baby boy."

There was a pure joy that filled me at the sound of his voice. "Hi, alpha."

"You didn't come to bed."

"What bed would that be?" I pinned him with a stare.

"The nest."

I sighed; I was tired of this already. "You mean Penelope's nest."

"I thought you were sharing."

"No, Richie decided that I was." Whatever Xavier was going to say next was cut off by a hissing sound from behind me, letting me know the forge was ready. I didn't have the energy or a fuck to give for this conversation right now.

Standing, I grabbed the tongs and a couple of ingots of titanium. They found their home in one of the crucibles. I turned around and Xavier was already there with the single steel ingot, he flowed past me in a practiced dance, coming up to the open fire and dropping the metal into the second crucible. "Do you really think weapon crafting while upset is the best idea?"

"I do my best work when I'm pissed off."

His laugh caught me by surprise. "So, you are mad. Why?"

"I just feel out of control. I need to claim it back," I admitted.

"Are you going into heat?"

I almost laughed at his implication. "Not for at least a month. I just don't feel settled."

Xavier nodded, seeming to understand what I meant without me needing to voice it. He took my hand and led me to the forge, there was something very intimate about the way he stood just behind me, boxing me in. His head came down, burying his nose in my hair and inhaling. "You always smell so damn good, baby boy."

"I've been working out all day. God knows there's not much else I can do. I'm a pampered, spoiled little omega after all."

"Who ever accused you of being little?"

I spun in his arms. "I believe you did, alpha. The last time we had sex."

"When was that precisely?"

"About two weeks ago," I huffed. "Which, by the way, is part of the problem."

"Surely someone else has..."

"No one has touched me in the last two weeks. In fact, you're the only one that has in a long time."

"Bradley had to have." He was so sure of himself.

"It's been nearly a month."

"Evan?"

"When I got tattooed."

"Richie?"

There was hope in his voice. I pegged him with a stare that would have wilted flowers. "I can't remember the last time he looked at me let alone touched me."

"We need to fix that." I ignored him and pulled out of his arms so I could grab the metal before it got too hot.

I reached down for the iron I used to pull the molten metal. Dipping the end into the well of titanium in the center of the coals, I pulled a large enough ball to work with. Using my tongs, I grabbed some of the metal. Pinning it to the table as I worked. Xavier came around, having slid on gloves and an apron, he grabbed tongs from my hand and nodded at me. I released my hold and started to back up, twisting the glob as I pulled, making the handle of the axe with every movement. My free hand dropped until I was able to wrap it around the shears and cut the excess off. Pushing the iron forward, I capped off the end of the handle.

It had already started to cool into a beautiful silver color. As much as I would love to keep it that color, it would need to be anodized, turning it more of a deep metallic purple. I was just starting to pull a smaller ball of titanium when Evan came in. "Dante, my love."

He was already pulling on his gloves and apron as he came over to me. Pressing a kiss to my cheek, he went over to the table and took a place next to Xavier. I was already moving, collecting another dab of metal on the tip of the iron. Coming back to the table, I smiled when I saw that Evan already had the end of the handle gripped in the tongs. He was looking up at me expectantly, waiting for instruction. That was what I always loved about my pack. They always took care of me until we came to the smithy. This was my territory. The only place where my word reigned supreme. And I loved that they trusted me so completely.

"Spin the handle as I lay the metal." He started to slowly move the handle as I held the molten liquid over it.

He held it in place long enough for it to start to cool as it pooled before he started to spin. Xavier worked along the other side of the table, guiding the molten substance with a metal scoop. Working the handle behind me, he guided the molten metal into the perfect shape. This was me in my element, my men working in tandem with me to create beautiful but deadly works of art. The metal was dripping at a steady rate allowing me to create a unique grip pattern that would make the handle less likely to slip when covered in blood. When I made it to the bottom, I still had half the glob left. I moved back up to the top of the handle, letting a platform build up. Xavier took a wet stack of paper in his hand, guiding the newspaper over the flat end. His hands moved, helping me create the platform in just the right way to provide enough support to the blade.

I pulled the iron back when I was satisfied and buried it into the crucible of steel, stirring the metal for a moment before turning back to the table. Evan was quenching the handle in a bucket of oil. The flames dancing along the top of the liquid told me as much. He was moving before the fire died out, pulling it from the barrel and submerging it into one filled with water. There was a hissing that I ignored. We worked like that well into the night, their silent acceptance that I was refusing to acknowledge the real problem here was everything I needed at the moment. I spent hours sculpting the blade so it fit my vision just right. By the time I was done, it was a gnarly weapon that still needed its edge, or edges, considering there were smaller spurs of metal that I intended to sharpen.

"Time for bed." Evan called it a night before I could. They helped me pull off the protective gear before leading me out of the smithy to his room. Xavier was right there with us, picking me up when I stumbled and carrying me the rest of the way to Evan's room.

"Don't want sleep. I want a knot." I murmured, half asleep as Xavier laid me down on the bed.

"If you can remain standing for thirty seconds I'll give you just what you want." There was a challenge in his voice I just couldn't ignore. I started to roll over, nearly coming to my feet when Xavier knelt there, his hair was down, the tips of his locs kissing his shoulders as he looked down at me. "You really want your alpha's knot?" That was all I needed to be wide awake.

I reached for him, my hands catching his shirt. My grip was steady as I pulled him in, our lips met, and I let every last bit of what I was feeling into it. I needed him, needed him more than I ever had before. "Mine."

"Always, baby boy."

"Prove it." It was a challenge that I issued to both men in the room.

Chapter 15

Evan

Listening to Dante challenge me and Xavier was the sexiest thing I had heard in a long time. The alpha was already moving, lifting Dante, and stripping his clothes with one hand. I marveled at how hot they looked together. Dante was small in the alpha's grasp, and Xavier's large hands made the omega look even smaller. Everything about the scene made my mouth water, my cock hard and leaking at the thought of seeing them together. Xavier was devastatingly handsome, dedicated to Dante's pleasure as he was. There was only one thing I could think of that would make this better.

Moving to my desk, I grabbed my camera from inside, checking the battery and the memory. I was glad when I saw it was ready for use. I was headed back to the bed, camera in hand, stripping as I moved. Xavier and Dante were looking up at me as if they were waiting for me to return. Lifting the camera to my eye, I focused on their faces as their lips met. Their eyes were closed, tongues dancing. Dante's hand was buried between Xavier's locs, holding the alpha close to him. I snapped three pictures in quick succession. Xavier pulled back, kissing his way down the omega's throat. He paused at his mark, nipping at it made Dante throw his head back. I snapped another picture then.

The alpha's hand slid between Dante's legs, wrapping his hand around the omega's cock. I came around until I was standing by the omega's head. His hands came up, tugging at my pants until my cock fell out. Leaning over, he lapped at me. When his eyes moved up to look at me, I took another picture. My free hand came down to play with his hair as he suckled on my head. Xavier moved next to Dante, his tongue lashing out to tease my balls. I hissed at the feeling as I shifted enough to catch both of them in frame.

They moved in tandem, switching over so the alpha was swallowing my cock, inch by inch. Dante moved, kissing his way up my chest. Lifting the camera over my head I aimed it down and took a selfie with both of them. I was leaking by the time Xavier pulled back, my hand found the back of his head, fisting his locs as I fucked his face. He growled around me, his arms wrapping around my hips to keep me buried in his throat. "Fuck, alpha."

His hand moved, coming up to wrap around my throat and pull me to my knees. I moved with him, falling forward until I was resting on the bed beside him. Knowing what he wanted, I spun around so we were facing the same direction. Our heads turned to the side as one, our lips meeting in an explosion of lust. His tongue slid past my lips, our kiss deepening until I was moaning for him. I felt Dante's lips on my neck as he kissed his way down my chest. He moved and I felt coolness on my cock as the omega stroked me with lube. Xavier's hands slid up my body, teasing my nipples until I throbbed for him. Warmth encompassed my cock making me pull back from the kiss.

Struggling to catch my breath, my gaze shifted to the omega who was currently riding me. My hands slid up his thighs until I was holding his waist, I could feel the muscles flexing beneath his skin as I held him in place. Pulling out slowly, he squirmed for me when I slammed home. His cock throbbing, slick leaking from the tip with each stroke. His cinnamon roll scent filling the air. I loved it, my mouth watering as I reached to collect some of it on my fingers. When they were soaked , I brought them to my lips. The minute the liquid touched my tongue, my cock throbbed, my eyes rolling into the back of my head as I moaned from the sweet ambrosia that was his slick. The taste of him was enough to make me explode, my cock throbbing as I filled my omega with my cum.

His cock throbbed as he soaked my stomach with his cum. That sweet scent thickened. My abs tensed when I felt a tongue on my stomach collecting the omega's seed. When I opened my eyes, I saw Xavier nearing me, joy clearly on his face. Our lips met, his tongue sliding inside me. He deposited that sweet cum there, making me moan and throb again. Our kiss deepened as we shared our omega's seed between us. We both swallowed as we pulled back, turning to Dante where he was still impaled. Xavier leaned forward, catching the omega's hips, and lifting him off me. He shifted, bringing Dante to sit just above his cock.

Our omega's knees shifted as he impaled himself on Xavier. The alpha's moan was enough to make me shoot hard again. Xavier had the camera now and was pointing it up at Dante as he rode the alpha's cock. From that angle he would be able to get all of Dante. I could see the picture now, Dante leaning back, the alpha's cock disappearing inside him, Xavier's knot just starting to stretch the omega. Dante's cock throbbed, leaking his slick onto the alpha's stomach.

I was behind Dante in a flash, my cock in my hand. "Sweet little omega, you want both our cocks, don't you?"

"Please." I was teasing him with just the head of me, stretching him until he collapsed on top of Xavier.

I slid inside him just a little. Xavier's voice whispered encouragement into Dante's ear. "You got this, baby boy." He kissed our omega on the cheek, helping him relax. I slid a few more inches inside him, his moan making me throb. "You're being such a good boy for Daddy."

"Daddy..." he moaned between us. He relaxed even more until I was balls deep inside him, "I need..."

"Tell us what you need." I needed his words now more than ever.

"Move, please."

"You heard our omega." Xavier moved first, his length sliding against mine until I could feel his head against the base of my cock. Pushing forward, he filled Dante, our heads sliding against the other until we were both leaking. My hips moved on instinct, dragging myself out of him until I could feel his knot against my head. "You're taking us so well."

We found our rhythm easily, timing our thrusts so he was filled with us at all times. His first orgasm came crashing down, tightening around us until we both had to push against him to stay inside. When he relaxed, we slipped into that rhythm again until I was fighting not to fill him. Xavier drug his cock against mine one last time, his thrust making me spill inside Dante. I collapsed on top of our omega sandwiching him between us. I heard a click and looked up to see Xavier holding the camera in the air.

"I need..." Dante's voice was all it took for me to move. Catching the camera in my hand, I came back to my knees, keeping my cock buried inside him.

Xavier leaned forward, nibbling on Dante's earlobe before whispering, "You want your alpha's knot?"

"Please." That was enough for me to pull out of him. When I spilled from the omega Xavier pushed forward, filling Dante with his knot. The alpha's moans followed me to the bathroom as I wet a few washcloths to clean us all up. By the time I came back into the room they had rolled to the side and Xavier was playing with Dante's hair. I could hear Dante say, "Time for sleep," before his eyes closed, his breath evening out. He was asleep before I could make it to the bed.

Chapter 16

Penelope

There was something strange about being back in this house—this nest—that I couldn't quite place. I was essentially a stranger to these men. I certainly wasn't the same woman I was when I ran from them. Seven long years had passed since then and I certainly wasn't the same people-pleaser that I used to be. There was something missing and I knew just what it was. Dante should have been here with us. This nest was created with both of us in mind, I could make that much out from the way it was designed. There was so much extra space here that just needed to be filled. It almost felt like Dante was holding an open space for me. I knew that was too much to hope for, but I couldn't stop myself from wishing.

This was more my fault than anything. Running from Dante had done much more damage to him than I would have liked. And here I was, nearly a decade later, waltzing back in and acting like nothing had changed. But I knew that was anything but what I felt, it almost felt like he had rolled over and accepted he was losing his pack to me. That wasn't my intention at all, not that intent matters much. The impact of what was happening was plain for anyone to see. It was hard to miss the way the other omega's eyes tracked me as I walked, the way he got annoyed when his alphas were paying me any attention at all. That was a fair reaction, I had given up any right to this pack when I ran. I just wished I knew how to fix it. We couldn't go on like this, Dante certainly couldn't, it wasn't healthy for either of us. It was hard for me to see Dante so sad; he had been the happy one of us for years. If me being here was going to be a detriment to that, then I needed to go.

I would start making inquiries at omega safe apartment complexes tomorrow. For now, I needed to put my plan into motion. Richie was asleep to my right, his legs wrapped around mine, and Bradley was curled around me to my left. I wiggled until I was able to crawl free of them.

Coming to my feet, I took a moment to study the scene I had left behind on the bed. Richie grumbled, reaching over, and grabbing the pillow I had been laying on. He wrapped himself around it before settling back down. Bradley rolled over, his burgundy hair falling over his eyes. I was tempted to rejoin them in bed, but I needed to get this show on the road. My hands shook as I reached over and collected my phone from the nightstand before tiptoeing across the room and pulling open the door.

Sliding into the hallway, I closed it behind me as quietly as I could, praying that I didn't wake Richie up. I made it to the kitchen when the ringing of my phone made me jump. The number wasn't one that I had saved, and I almost didn't answer it, but curiosity got the better of me.

"Didn't wake you, did I?" Rhys asked when I answered it.

"How did you even get this number?"

There was something in his laugh that made me wet. "Wouldn't you like to know?"

"Yes, I would, that's why I asked."

"It doesn't matter." I could hear rustling behind him and a muffled voice.

"You're literally killing someone right now."

"I am doing no such thing." His denial was too quick to be anything but the truth. "That's not why I called you anyway."

"This time."

"Yes, this time. I have information for you."

"How do I know this isn't a trick to get me alone so you can kill me?"

"I had that opportunity the other night." There wasn't even a hint of threat in his voice. "And as I told you then, you are mine, and I never hurt what is mine." I didn't even know how to respond to that. "I'm going to give you directions, meet me there and I'll tell you everything."

"I don't trust you."

"Good, you shouldn't." He proceeded to give me the most convoluted directions I had ever heard. If I was understanding him right, this would put me out in the middle of a nature preserve. He didn't give me time to question him, hanging up as soon as he was done.

My mind was racing a mile a minute, there were so many things that could go wrong, but I needed to take the chance. Scanning the kitchen, I chuckled when I spotted the keys hanging from the hooks by the garage door. I chose one at random, pulling open the garage door and hitting the unlock button. I sprinted across the room, pulling open the driver's side door of the black 1967 Chevy Impala as soon as the aftermarket alarm beeped. I couldn't help but chuckle as I realized this had to be Richie's car. He was the only one of the pack that knew a single thing about classic cars. I was just climbing in when I heard Richie's voice. "Where are we going?"

Chapter 17

Richie

There was an empty space between me and Bradley. It was the lack of warmth that woke me up, telling me something was wrong. Sitting up, I scanned the nest, realizing that, once again, Dante had chosen not to sleep with us. I needed to have a talk with him soon about his attitude with Penelope. He had kept his distance from all of us since she came into the house, all but surrendering his nest to the other omega. It was a sweet gesture, at least I thought it was. That was until he stopped sleeping here with the pack immediately after Penelope got here.

He was going to have to get over himself, Penelope wasn't going anywhere. Getting out of bed, I went into the living room, there was nothing there either. I almost went back to bed when I heard a sound from the garage. Finding my way there, I slid into the room, the overhead light blinding me for a moment. When my vision cleared, I spotted Penelope climbing into the driver's seat of my car. I couldn't help but laugh. She had good taste, but it was the worst car she could have chosen if she was running from us again.

I came around the passenger side as she cranked it, her head was turned opposite me as I reached up and opened the door, sliding into the seat beside her. "Where are we going?"

She jumped, her momentary weakness was sexy in a way I didn't know what to do with. "Jesus, Richie, say something before you come out of nowhere."

"I figured you didn't want to get caught sneaking out."

"Yeah, but now that I'm busted, we can just go back to bed."

"You had a plan." I leaned over, looking at the navigation app she had open on her phone. "So, where are we headed?"

She sighed, putting the car in reverse and backing us out of the driveway. Turning the car toward the mountains, we drove in silence for a while. Part of me wanted to insist we turn around, force her to take us back to the safety of the house. But there was a larger part of me that was more than curious. I needed to find out what she was thinking, how she was feeling. She was ravishing, her black curls kissing her shoulders. Blue eyes turned on me when she spoke, "I'm going hunting."

"Hunting...for?"

"I need you to answer some questions." She took a breath before continuing. "I need to know I can trust you."

"Does this have to do with why you left us?"

She pulled to the side of the road, putting the car into park before turning to stare at me. "You really have no idea why I left, do you?"

"None of us do." We had been dancing around this conversation for the last two months since she moved in with us. "If it's something we did, you need to tell me."

"There's nothing you can do about the family you were born into."

"Explain."

The sound she released resembled a growl. "Don't bark at me, asshole."

"Am I an asshole or are you just not making any sense?"

"You can't be sweet to me." She was using her hair to hide, allowing it to fall over her face. "I won't be able to walk away again if you are."

All my indignation fled when she said that. "Talk to me, raven."

"Why raven?"

"Edgar Allen Poe couldn't get rid of that damned raven, and you will never get rid of me."

Her laugh made warmth build in my gut. "That would make you the raven and me the poet."

"Doesn't matter. Tell me why you ran from us, from me."

"You know my birth mother was murdered."

It was such an abrupt change of subject that I was stunned for a moment. "You never really wanted to talk about it."

"The man who killed her escaped from prison."

"Fuck." That was the moment it all clicked. "You didn't tell me."

"You didn't say anything either."

I rolled my eyes. "What am I supposed to say? *I love you; can't wait to have you bear my mark. Oh, by the way, my stepbrother, Rhys Kelly, tortured and killed people for fun.* Yeah, that flows right off the tongue."

"Yeah, as if, *your stepbrother killed my mother* rolls off the tongue any better."

"So, you ran from me." She turned her head from me, not wanting to give me her eyes as we talked. I was having none of it, reaching over and getting a grip on her chin. I pulled her face until she was looking at me. "Don't do that again. Losing you once was a hard enough blow for me. I will not tolerate it happening again. Run from me again and I will hunt you down and you will be sorry when I do."

"What do you want from me?"

"Admit you're mine." That was all I needed from her.

I was so sure I pushed her as far as she would allow until she leaned forward and caught my lips with hers. The kiss was tentative at first, as if she wasn't sure of herself. I ached to reach up and wrap my hand around her throat, pull her closer and claim her once and for all. I stilled myself, relinquishing my control to her. It went against everything I knew about being an alpha. She needed this and I loved to give her what she needed. As if sensing my hesitancy, she leaned in, deepening the kiss. My cock reacted, growing, throbbing hard. When she pulled back she was breathless. "Fuck."

"My thoughts exactly."

"You don't hate me?"

"My raven." I leaned forward and pressed a kiss to her forehead. "I could never hate you."

She leaned back in the seat, seeming content to let the moment pass. Pulling back onto the highway, she gunned the engine to get back up to speed. We sat in silence for a while as I watched the trees fly by. We were on a section of the road between towns when she pulled off onto a dirt road. The confident way she drove down the road made me uneasy. There was nothing around us but forest for miles.

"You aren't taking me out here to kill me, are you?" I was half teasing her.

"Someone might die tonight, rest assured, if I wanted you dead I don't have to leave the house."

That wasn't comforting. "So, who are you here to kill?"

"I don't know yet." She got out of the car as we reached a cabin in the middle of a large clearing. I followed quickly, not wanting to let her out of my sight. "I found one of the men that escaped with your stepbrother. I just want to ask him some questions."

She was hiding something from me, and I couldn't tell what it was. I couldn't risk losing her again by pushing her for something she wasn't ready for, so I said the only thing I could, "Fine, but I go in first." She allowed me to pass her. Tension filled me, not knowing what I was going to find behind that door. I hated the idea that an escaped convict was going to be so close to my omega; the danger she was going to be in from that alone. Pushing the door open, I stopped when I saw the omega that was sitting there. I hadn't ever seen him in person, but I recognized him from the pictures that Devyn shared at our meetings. "Liam, does Devyn know you escaped?"

"How do you know this omega?" I was shocked for a moment when I saw Rhys standing there beside Liam.

"Rhys." I felt Penelope tense behind me, her hands clutching the back of my shirt like I was the only thing keeping her from falling.

"Richie. I've always thought that was the most asinine name, but what can you do about it?"

"What do you want?" I was so close to charging him, but I couldn't until I figured out a way to get both omegas out of here.

"You have something that belongs to me."

I rolled my eyes. "What would that be?"

"My omega." Penelope gasped behind me, drawing his attention to her. "Is she hiding behind you?"

"Don't speak to my omega." My growl came out before I could stop it, a clear threat to my stepbrother.

"The only thing I'm a threat to is her throat, or maybe her wrist, I haven't decided exactly where I'm putting my mark yet, and rest assured, she will be wearing it." He seemed too sure of himself.

Penelope chose that moment to step out from behind me. "You aren't coming anywhere near me. If you even think of it I will bury one of my axes in your brain."

"A feisty one." His laugh was eerily familiar. "I like that. Now tell me how you know this omega."

"He is mated to a close friend of mine. Well, his twin."

"You know Devyn?" Liam was excited, as if he was realizing for the first time he was being taken care of again.

"I do." I nodded. "I can call him if you'd like. Tell him where you are."

"Yes, please." His eyes lit up at the thought.

Reaching into my pocket, I retrieved my phone and called the club owner. It rang a few times before he picked it up. The racket of the club behind him made me hesitate to say anything. For all I knew he was having an auction tonight, and I couldn't interrupt that. He would be pissed if I did. "What do you want?"

"Do you know where your omega is?"

"Fuck, I can't hear you. Give me a moment." There was shuffling as he moved through his club. Soon, there was a very final sounding click as he closed himself in his office. "What was that?"

"I asked if you knew where your omega was."

"You know damn well we lost him years ago." I knew the story well. We had gotten him to share one drunken night. Seems they had formed a pack in college, but one of them had a twin that sold their omega.

"You should really keep better track of what's yours."

He growled. "Did you just call me to taunt me?"

I sighed, the only way to deal with this was to just spit it out. "I found him."

"Fuckin' what?"

"I found your precious omega." I was getting bored with this conversation. "Did you know he was in prison?"

"Excuse the fuck out of me?"

"Yeah, apparently he escaped with my stepbrother and one other convicted serial killer." There wasn't much else to say.

"I don't believe you."

I pulled up the camera app, leaning around to the opening and snapping a quick picture of the male omega. "Pretty sure that's the omega you've been looking for."

There was silence as he checked the message I sent him. "Tell me where to go."

I gave him the information, there was nothing else I could do. "When should I expect you?"

"Soon." There was a muffled conversation as if he had put his hand over the receiver. "How about some quid pro quo?"

"Oh?"

"We have a lead on Amani." I froze when I heard Xavier's sister's name.

My phone dinged before I could process what I had just been told. Pulling it from my ear, I checked the message. It was from Devyn with a picture of a beautiful Black woman, she couldn't have been a day over twenty-five. There was no telling what she had been through. "Where is she?"

"We don't know just yet," Devyn admitted.

I hung up, turning back to the omegas and Rhys. "Devyn will be here soon."

Chapter 18

Rhys

Being so close to the omega of my dreams and not being able to touch her was agony. She was terrified of me, I could tell that from the way her white chocolate scent soured as soon as we were alone. Or maybe that was anger, that made more sense considering I told her I killed her parents' pack. Either way, I adored the way she was looking at me, like she was measuring me for a casket. That shadow in her eyes made my cock hard. I recognized that darkness, it was so like the one I carried inside me, a threat and warning to all around. She was planning my death, that much I was sure of.

"What are you staring at?" Her snapping at me said she had more fight in her than I expected.

"I would say an omega I could sink my teeth into, but that would be kind of obvious." I reached down to adjust my cock where it was pressing against my jeans.

The look she gave me was one of pure disgust. That would change in time, even if I had to force her to come around. In my family, there were stories, familial legends, really, about an alpha finding his fated omega. It was said that when an alpha found their fated one, they knew in several ways. It all started with the senses. Sometimes they saw their mate and it was as if the world narrowed down to that person. That was certainly happening with me and Penelope. All I could see was her pale skin, the way her cerulean eyes stared at me through the black curls that fell across her face. My eyes traveled down her body, taking in the swell of her breasts, moving down to take in her plump waist. The curve of her hips made me want to hold her tight, watch the way her skin moved as it pushed against my hold.

Sound was the next to go, normally, but I knew Penelope was mine the moment I heard her voice. I started to reach for her, but I was stopped by Liam's hand on my arm. "Stay here."

I looked down at the omega, pausing long enough for his hand to tighten on my arm. When I looked back up, Richie had joined us again. At his side was another alpha that made Liam's breath freeze in his chest. My growl came without warning as the other alpha started to approach us. He was being cautious—not careful enough if you asked me. "That's close enough."

"Alpha." Liam's voice was small next to me. I was hesitant to allow this alpha anywhere near him.

There was pain in the man's voice when he spoke again. "I never thought I would see you again."

"The plan was to sell me."

"It was."

"Flynn sold me, you're just mad he got to it before you did." Liam snapped. "Now where is my alpha and why have *you* come for me and not him?"

"We lost you."

"You lost me." Liam crossed the room and smacked the alpha. "You really expect me to believe you couldn't find me when I was in a federal prison. My prints were on file for fucks sake!"

"You have to believe me." Devyn approached, but my growl stopped him in his tracks. "We tried to find you. Tried to save you. We were one step behind you the whole time. Until you disappeared. We thought you were dead."

"Flynn knew. Where is my alpha?" The panic in Liam's voice made me want to reach out and strangle Devyn.

The door slammed open as I watched a double of Devyn come in. As similar as they looked, they couldn't be more different. Devyn just had an aura of weakness, while Flynn had a strength about him that I recognized all too well. His eyes were as dead as mine as he spoke. "I suggest you stop scaring my omega before I make myself an only child."

Liam took off running from my side. I was close behind, closing the distance between us at a steadier pace. The omega threw himself into the alpha's arms, burrowing into his coat and letting out a sigh of contentment. The alpha nodded at me. "Rhys."

He shifted Liam enough so he could offer me a hand. "Thank you for finding him for me."

"I couldn't leave him where he was." I would never tell this man the way Liam's screams tore at me. How I was nearly driven insane from not being able to help him.

"You're better than most people."

"The things they were doing to him..."

"You care for my omega." There was a dangerous edge to his voice.

"I do." I nodded. "But he is not mine."

The other alpha turned and started to carry the omega out of the house. Liam said something to Flynn, making the alpha release a deep rumbling growl. He turned around and gave me eyes filled with the promise of my death. If that was the case, he could bring it on. "Liam said he would like if you would stay in contact with him."

I nodded before handing him a phone. "I got this for Liam anyway. My number is programmed."

Chapter 19

Penelope

I couldn't relax until I was back in the car. Richie was behind the wheel, turning it toward the house. I wasn't ready to go back there; I needed time to think. Someone to talk to. Pulling out my phone, I texted Amani, hoping that she would be able to meet with me tonight. She was always the voice of reason, I could use a little of that right now. Thankfully, she responded, telling me to come over.

"Turn right up here." I directed the alpha.

He looked over at me before nodding and following every one of my directions until he pulled up in front of the shelter. "You seriously expect me to allow you to go in there?"

"I was going to invite you in with me." I tossed my hair over my shoulder as I watched Dorian approach the driver's side of the car. "But if you're going to be like that you can stay out here with her alpha."

His head turned and I got to see the shock play across his face as he watched Dorian coming. "Fine."

I sat in the car until Richie came around, opening the door for me. Dorian was there, offering his hand to me. I allowed him to help me out of the car and lead me into the building. He went to the office, swinging a file cabinet to the side, revealing a set of stairs that led into the basement. I was through the small opening before Richie could protest. My laughter at his calling after me carried me into the basement rooms where Amani and Dorian lived.

Coming around the corner, I spotted Amani sitting on her couch, scrolling through her phone. She looked up at me when I entered, a smile crossing her face. "God damn it, Penelope, you should know better than to run ahead of me." I watched that smile drop from her eyes when she heard Richie's voice.

"You didn't tell me he was with you."

"I'm sorry." I turned, catching Richie's arm as he swept into the room. Pulling his head down, I whispered in his ear. "I'm trusting you here. Don't make me regret it."

"Amani." Richie's deep voice was enough to make anyone pay attention.

She held her face tight as she studied him. "Richie, I don't suppose you'll forget you ever saw me."

"I can't promise to never tell him." Dorian's growl at Richie's words made my alpha pull me against his side. "But I can forget to mention it for a while."

I let out a sigh. Coming from Richie, that was as good as a promise. Amani knew that. "I know you must have questions."

"Not unless you're in the mood to tell me."

That was the perfect answer, making the other alpha relax back against the couch. Dorian crossed the room and pulled her into his arms, her head came to rest on his shoulder. His hand moved, collecting her silver box braids, starting to braid them into an intricate up-do. I smiled knowing this was part of their nightly ritual. He leaned forward, grabbing her bonnet and handing it to her. She was more relaxed than I had ever seen her when she sat up, taking it from him and putting it on.

He grabbed her cigarette box, lighting one of the spliffs and handing it to her. She pressed a gentle kiss to his cheek before turning back to me and saying, "You wanted to talk, so talk."

"I ran into Rhys."

"The man who murdered your mother?"

"Yeah, that's him." I nodded.

"Tell me everything." I hesitated, not wanting to admit everything I felt. I hated feeling this way, not wanting to tell my best friend everything was a strange concept. My eyes moved to Richie. Him being here was making me hesitate. Seeing it, Amani asked, "Dorian, can you take Richie to collect the blankets that need to be washed?"

The alpha took the hint, leading Richie out of the room and leaving me alone with her. "He's not anything like I expected him to be."

"Well?"

"I expected a serial killer to look more dangerous. Like a monster."

"And he didn't?"

"No, he was kind of cute actually." The admission made me blush.

"Cute?!"

"Yes, cute." He was that, like, a boy next door grown into a man. He had the classic features that would make him attractive to nearly anyone. When he stood, his head nearly brushed the ceiling, he had to be close to seven feet tall. And boy did he look cuddly. "And he was so confident that anyone would want him."

"You want him though."

That was a statement. "I don't."

"You can lie to Richie and yourself all you want but you can't lie to me."

"Fine," I hissed. "I do want him. I shouldn't, but I do."

"Now that you've admitted that, how do you think your pack will take it?"

"They aren't my pack." The denial came too quickly from my lips for it to be the truth. "And even if they were, I wouldn't bring a serial killer home to them."

"Home, huh?" The blush creeping up my chest was enough to give me away.

My phone rang as we sat there. When I pulled it out of my pocket I saw it was from an unknown number. I answered it on speaker with, "Can I help you?"

"If you wish to keep your tongue in that head of yours, I suggest you never take that tone with me again." The voice on the other end was not Rhys.

"I must apologize, I thought you were someone else. How can I help you?"

Flynn's voice made me sit up straight. "Is it true you are friends with a woman who runs a shelter?"

"I don't know who you're talking about." The look of panic in Amani's eyes was enough for me to protect her at all costs.

"You would do better not to lie to me."

"Why does something I don't even have matter so much?"

The silence from the other end of the phone was terrifying. "My omega isn't doing well. I'd suggest you stop talking in circles"

"Then you need to call a doctor."

"I called you for a reason."

Amani made a hand gesture in the air as if indicating for me to keep him talking. "Give me a reason to trust you."

"My omega says you probably don't know him, but you know of him."

"You should really expand on that." I was doing everything I could to keep the man on the phone.

"Tell your friend that my omega was known as The Conqueror."

Amani pulled the phone from my hand, answering him, "Anyone who knows The Conqueror is welcome here." She gave him the address before handing the phone back to me.

"We need to get the guys back here." There was nervousness on my face as she nodded to me.

Chapter 20

Richie

Dorian was staring out of the front door as we waited for two unknown people to pull into the parking lot. I couldn't take the waiting, the not knowing. Dorian turned his head to the side, taking in the bored look on my face. "It's less boring if you make a game out of it."

"I never expected that protecting a shelter would take so much waiting."

His laugh brought a smile to my face. "It's mostly waiting, if I'm honest. Occasionally there's some asshole that doesn't like one of his omegas finally has had enough of his shit. But mostly waiting and looking threatening."

"I don't know why you do this."

"When you love someone who is in this line of work you do whatever you have to do to keep them happy."

I nodded. "What do you know about this conqueror guy?"

"For years there have been rumors of people killing traffickers. No one could ever get a lead on who was doing it, or if it was even happening. But, every once in a while, we will get someone who comes through mentioning The Conqueror and how they were saved by him." Headlights pulling in drew our attention to the attached lot, leaving Dorian's voice to trail off as we tracked the car's movements.

There was something familiar about the alpha that approached the door, and the omega tucked under his arm. I wasn't sure who it was until Dorian was pulling the door open for them. "Flynn."

"Richie, this is the last place I expected you to be." His voice held every bit of threat I knew he felt.

"You called my omega. Why the fuck wouldn't I be here?"

He nodded before turning to the omega I realized was Liam when he stepped into the light. "Go with Richie. He'll take you to the others."

Flynn pressed a gentle kiss to Liam's forehead before the omega came to my side. I turned, leading him back into the office. Amani and Penelope were sitting there as if they were waiting for just this moment. Amani stood, going to Liam, and taking his hands in hers. She led him deeper into the room until they disappeared down the stairs, Penelope smiled at me, blowing me a kiss before following them down to the basement.

Chapter 21

Xavier

There was something wrong, and I knew it as soon as I woke up. Dante was still sleeping in my arms, the space he had occupied for as long as I could remember. He had been touchier lately, often clinging to me like I was the only safe person he had in his life. That was probably truer than either of us cared to admit. He needed me now more than ever and I felt like I was failing him.

I could feel the sadness radiating off him when he watched the way the others were with Penelope, the way he shrunk in on himself whenever she was the center of attention. I was watching my pack fracture around me, and it was time it stopped. Rolling over, I pulled Dante into my arms, holding him close to me was the only comfort. The others had all but abandoned him, and I knew he was feeling the rejection whether he wanted to admit it or not. I couldn't stand that he was hurting. It made me want to rage at my pack, claim control of the pack from Bradley and set it all right. Dante was our center; the pack would survive our little alpha showdown. Then I could take care of my omega the way he deserved. I couldn't stay there, I needed to move.

Climbing out of the bed, I slid my pillow into my place. Dante's arms tightened around it before Evan pulled the omega against his chest. I closed my door as quietly behind me as I could and headed down the hall. Smelling Penelope's scent permeating from Dante's nest made me so angry. It was completely unfair; Dante stayed with us when Penelope ran. He was here, holding this pack together, when all that was left was tattered pieces of what we once were. He broke down the walls that everyone erected when she rejected them. Dante was a god to me, and I loved to worship him as he should be. This entire situation had me unsettled, and I hated knowing that she was making him feel like a stranger in his own home.

I had been sleeping in my workout shorts, so I headed to the gym in the basement. I wasn't at all surprised when I saw the light was already on.

Pushing through those doors, I was hit with Bradley's minty scent. He was jogging on one of the treadmills. From the amount of his scent that was in the air I would say he was on his cool down. That gave me plenty of time to have a long conversation with the other alpha. Neither of us spoke as I climbed onto the stationary bike next to him. Peddling until I was up to a steady speed, I spoke for the first time. "You know Dante's heat is due any time now."

"I'm aware."

"I'm surprised you cared to notice."

He turned so he was staring at me. I didn't bother to look at him, watching him in my peripheral as I started to sweat. His voice was starting to rumble as he spoke again. "I know everything about my omega."

"And which one is that?"

"I know who belongs to me."

"Are you sure of that?" I finally turned my head, giving him the full weight of my eyes. When he nodded, I continued. "Then why did Penelope move into his nest like she owned it? Why hasn't he shared a bed with all of us the way we used to? Why does he feel like a stranger in his own house?"

"He said all of that?"

I watched as his so- carefully- constructed world crumbled around him. Guilt started to creep up my spine. I was able to force the feeling down, knowing I was doing what was best for Dante. "He hasn't needed to. The nest smells so much like her I don't even want to go in there. I can't even imagine how Dante feels. Add to that Richie and your scents mixing with hers, it must be driving him insane. Why would he want to touch any of us when we all allowed that to happen?"

"He offered her his nest."

"Did he?" I pushed. "Or did Richie just do what he wanted and not care what anyone said? This is Penelope we' re talking about."

"Fuck."

I nodded. "Exactly."

"Where has Dante been sleeping?"

"With me."

He had a few more choice words for the situation before taking a breath. "How do we fix this?"

"You had a chance to fix this and yet you kept fucking it up."

"I know, I don't know what's wrong with me."

He looked genuinely sad about that. "Well, it's my problem now, my pack."

"I hope you do a better job than I did."

"I have a plan." I watched hope spring in his eyes again.

We spent the next half an hour hashing out the logistics. Heading to the nest, I was relieved to find it empty. I ticked off the things I needed to do to get it back in order. It wouldn't take much. We had brand new linens in a closet in the hall, I stopped and grabbed those. I hesitated for a moment before handing the sheets to Bradley and pulling out the new pillows. My nose wrinkled when I pushed the doors to the nest open. There was only one option for airing out the room, I pulled the fans from the closet and set them up in front of the windows. Moving to the bedside table, I opened a drawer and pulled out a remote that opened them. As they opened, Bradley turned on the fans one by one.

I moved to the bed and started to strip it. Every piece of it smelled like her and it all needed to go. I was frantic to get rid of the offending scent. Pillows, blankets, sheets, and the mattress cover went flying over my head. Spinning around, I smiled when Bradley was already there with the new sheets. He went around the opposite side of the bed and we moved as one to make it. The fresh pillows found their homes and I sighed.

There was only one thing I needed. One thing that Dante needed. "I'll be right back."

I went to Bradley's room first. My first instinct was to reach for the blanket. When I clutched it in my hands Bradley's scent had faded too much. The lack of it would have been a dead giveaway that he hadn't been sleeping here if I hadn't already known. That wouldn't do at all. My eyes scanned the room, looking for anything that might smell enough like him. I sighed with relief when I spotted his favorite hoodie lying on the floor. As soon as I picked it up, I was hit with his scent. It was a relief to check that off the list. The next stop was my room. I moved across the house as quietly as I could, trying not to wake Evan and Dante as I slid into my room which was right next to where my omega was sleeping. I headed right for the bed, grabbing the blanket and one of the pillows.

My arms were overly full, and I searched for a bag to put everything in. I found an old gym bag that I stuffed everything in. Heading to the bathroom, I grabbed the extra silk pillowcase and the durag that I would need to sleep in. Turning around, I reached beneath the cabinet and pulled out the extra bath bombs, lotions, scrubs, and all the things that Dante loved. It made my stash low, so I made a mental note to get more.

Running through my checklist, I made sure that I had everything Dante would need. When I was pleased, I left the room, pulling the door closed behind me with a satisfying click. I started to head for the nest, but something had me hesitating in front of Evan's door. Tempted as I was to go in there and get them both, I decided it was better to let them sleep for now.

Evan took that decision out of my hands, opening the door and almost walking right into me. It was kind of adorable how obviously frazzled he was.

When his eyes came up, I could see the relief in his azure gaze. "We have to do something; his heat is coming any day now."

"Come with me."

The beta caught up with me before I made it to the end of the hallway. I felt him coming at my back through the bond we shared. He was a moving bundle of stress, I made a note to do something about that later. Evan waited until we were far enough away from his room to ask, "What are we going to do about this?"

"We're reclaiming the nest."

"About fucking time," he sighed, relieved.

By the time we got back to the nest, the only thing I felt from Evan was a sense of calm. Pushing open the door, I was pleasantly surprised when it smelled like nothing but cleaning products. Those were lightly scented enough that they would quickly fade the more we used the room. Bradley looked up at me as we came in, relief plain on his face. "What's in the bag?"

"Goodies." I grinned as I moved to the bed. I opened the bag and upended it onto the bed. Everything fell out, bouncing on the mattress.

They sorted through the things on the bed, selecting what they wanted to give to Dante. I collected the rest and was stashing them beneath the bathroom sink when I heard the front door open. "Richie's going to be pissed," Evan whispered.

I could hear them coming up the steps. Making a snap decision, I filled the doorway, blocking their way. Penelope was leading Richie up the stairs, they both looked exhausted, but there was no way in hell I was letting either of them in the nest. Penelope stopped just before she ran into me. "There's a spare nest in the basement. I suggest you find it."

"Move." Richie's order came with so much arrogance behind it I wanted to reach out and throttle him.

"Not happening."

"Don't make me repeat myself." He was starting to get annoyed. I could feel him using his alpha aura, trying to force me to obey him, to submit to his will. That was never going to happen.

"Repeat yourself all you want. We are done letting you ruin this pack because you want to chase pussy."

Penelope looked insulted, making a pang of guilt hit my stomach. "Excuse me?!"

"That pout may work on Richie, but it does nothing for me. You aren't my omega."

Richie's growl was enough to make most of the alphas hide from him. I used to react that way. Now, I couldn't believe his audacity. "Don't speak to her that way."

"What way?" I stared at him with clear challenge in my eyes. "Like she's a guest who has overstepped her bounds? Because that's exactly what she is."

"We will see how Bradley and Evan feel about this."

"We support him," they chimed as one, yet there was a thread to their response that made me hesitate.

The redheaded alpha came up beside me, his head peeking out until he could see Penelope. "I moved the blankets, pillows and your stuff to the basement, darling. It's really where we should have settled you in the first place." He didn't wait for her reply before he turned around.

"Don't you care what our omega thinks about this?" I challenged Richie. "You know... Dante, the one you marked."

"I know he's here."

"So, when was the last time you slept in the same bed as him?" No response . "The last time you two cuddled?" Still nothing. "The last time you two fucked?"

"It was a few weeks ago, his last heat."

I crossed my arms, staring down at the other alpha. "That was nearly six months ago. Admittedly, you two only have sex once a month or so, but six months is excessive."

"It hasn't been... No, there's no way."

"Do you even know when his next heat is supposed to hit?"

He looked like he was doing trigonometry in his head before he answered. "Like... next month I think?"

"When is Penelope's?"

"Another week or two. You know these things aren't consistent, they come in cycles."

I shook my head. "Take *your* omega to the spare nest."

Penelope tried to argue, but Richie reached out and grabbed her wrist. He led her down the stairs and out of sight. My shoulders finally relaxed; I was finally able to breathe. Turning around, I walked back into the nest and closed the door behind me. Evan and Bradley looked at me expectantly. Shaking my head to clear it, I focused before speaking, "Go and get our omega."

Chapter 22

Dante

The bed was cold when I woke up, but there was warmth coming from the side of the bed that I rolled towards. Half-asleep, I needed whoever it was; my brain hadn't quite caught up yet. He pulled me into his arms surrounding me with his minty scent. That was enough to clear my brain. Looking up, I spotted Bradley holding me tight against his chest. I took a moment to appreciate him. He was the tallest of my alphas, needing to duck through doorways. His burgundy hair sat over piercing seafoam green eyes, with skin so pale you could see the blood rushing beneath it, lightly dusted with freckles. It all came together to make him striking. Many would have said he was dreamy; I preferred to call it a feminine masculinity that made me weak in the knees.

My own boy next door.

That's what he was in the truest sense. He had moved in next door to me and Calliope when we were five. He was nine, but we took an instant liking to each other. He was everything I didn't know I wanted in a man. Even then, he was protective and took care of me in ways neither of us had words for at the time. We grew up together, had the same friends, who eventually became my pack. Bradley, naturally, got his designation test first. When he came back as an alpha,

I was so excited for him, and full of hope for us. He was my first crush; I was incredibly lucky we became pack in the end.

But everything changed when I got my test results. We were so sure I was going to be a beta, never mind that twins rarely have different designations. I needed to be a beta. That was the only way things would have worked with all of us. Richie and Penelope had joined our little group by then. Penelope was our omega, it couldn't be me. That would ruin everything. Then, the results came in. I was an omega, there were no buts about it.

Bradley cradled me in his arms and started to move; I spoke before he got too far, "Where are you taking me?"

"To the nest."

"Why?"

"We have a surprise for you, little love." The rumble of his chest as he spoke was soothing to me, making me more at ease in his arms.

"I need blankets and pillows."

He smiled, turning around and lowering me down enough so I could snag what I wanted. The blanket and both pillows ended up in my lap. Bradley moved like a man on a mission, carrying me past the smithy and into the living room. We were at the nest door before I could get a handle on what was happening. The door was ajar, I held my breath, not wanting to smell Penelope in my space. I hated that she had been in my nest at all. My eyes scanned the room as Bradley carried me in, setting me on my feet as soon as we were inside. I was in shock at what my alphas and beta had done for me. My chest hurt from holding my breath, so I exhaled. When I inhaled, I sighed from relief; there was no scent but a faint one from the cleaner they used. There were fresh linens on the bed. All traces of the other omega had been erased from the room.

I should have been relieved, but I wasn't. Something was missing, and I knew just what it was. Not that I could voice that to my men, they had gone to all this trouble, I couldn't bring myself to comment. It was the sweetest thing that they had done for me, realizing that I was avoiding the nest. They were right about the reason too, but it had nothing to do with Penelope being here, or even in the nest itself. "Fuck."

"What is it, little one?" Xavier's voice made my head turn to look at him, his cobalt eyes were filled with adoration.

"I figured out what was wrong." I chewed on my bottom lip, debating telling them the truth. "It wasn't Penelope."

"You could have fooled me; you've been avoiding her like she has the plague."

I went to Xavier. "She rejected me."

"I know, little one."

"You're not an omega, you don't get it," I sighed.

"You're not like other omegas."

"In this, I think I am." My brain was moving a mile a minute, thoughts flying in and out of my head. "It's been nearly a decade, and now she's back. In my house. In my space."

My breaths came more rapidly as I started to overthink, the panic began to hit me full force. Xavier saw the worried look on my face and nodded. "Bradley, go get them."

He reached out before I could say anything, sweeping me off my feet and moving us back until I was curled up on the bed beside me. Evan came to lie on the other side, his arm fell across my lap to hold Xavier's hand. My head turned to look up at my alpha, I couldn't believe how lucky I was to have an alpha like him. He wasn't the tallest of my men, standing just slightly taller than me, but that was what made him my favorite. The size difference wasn't so much that it was uncomfortable. His rich thyme and rosemary scent made me feel like I was home every time I was around him. There was something very regal about the way he carried himself. Even now, in sleeping pants that hung from his hips just right and his lack of a shirt, he was positively glowing. He was everything I could ever want in a man. I wrapped myself around my alpha, leaning in until I could press a kiss to his throat. He purred for me, his rumble making me relax against him.

Our private moment was interrupted by the door opening. Richie entered first, scanning the room like a predator. Spotting me and the rest of the pack on the bed, he nodded before stepping to the side. Penelope came in with her head down, refusing to look at anyone. I hated her acting that way, scanning the room like everyone inside was a threat to her. Bradley came to the bed, sitting between me and Evan. Penelope hesitated, making Richie stay at her side. The pain of yet another rejection made my stomach twist.

I sat up, shrugging off Xavier's arm as I spoke to Penelope. "I must apologize for the way my alpha acted toward you. While he had good intentions, he did not have a full understanding of the situation."

"But he was right. I did come in here like I owned the place." Her head finally came up and she gave me the full weight of those blue eyes.

"Technically, you do."

Everyone was silent for a moment; Richie and I were the only ones who knew that little fact. She was on the deed, same as I was. The house was a courting gift from my men, it had everything I ever wanted in a home, including two nests. I had always intended to share it with Penelope, she just ran from me before I could. "You can't be serious."

I nearly laughed at her response. "You're on the deed with me."

"Why?"

"I always intended to share my life with you. You left before I could say anything."

"Oh, Dante." She came to me, crawling up the bed with the biggest shit-eating grin on her face. She sat between my legs in the place Bradley had vacated. "I hated leaving you."

"Then why did you?"

She looked over her shoulder at Bradley. When he nodded, she started to speak. "You know my mother was killed, but I never told you who did it."

Everyone was frozen in place, not reaching out to comfort the other omega. I couldn't take it and pulled her into my arms. Her head came to rest on my chest as I lay back into Evan and Xavier's arms. "Go on, princess."

"Rhys Kelly killed my mother."

"That's no reason to run from us."

The next thing I was going to say was cut off by Richie's booming voice. "It's my fault she left, actually."

"What did you do?" His eyes widened when I used that tone with him. "Don't lie to me, or you will be punished."

"It's not so much something I did."

He was hedging. I put more authority in my voice, channeling the dominant I was in the bedroom into the next words I spoke. "Out with it. Don't make me tell you again."

Chapter 23

Penelope

The whole mood had shifted when Dante started issuing orders. Their scents changed, becoming sweeter with anticipation. Richie's was the strongest to me, his scent becoming like warming clove tea. Richie winked at me before answering Dante. "There's a bit of a connection between me and Penelope that we didn't realize. She found out before I did, and she panicked."

"Stop being a brat or I'm not going to let you cum anytime soon."

"My omega might have something to say about that." I couldn't stop the blush that spread across my face when Richie claimed me in front of them. Even with the sexual tension in the room, we weren't entirely comfortable with each other. That was my fault, and it was time I owned it.

"Dante has a point. This is something we all should have been told about a long time ago. Considering it's the reason I left, it needs to be shared."

"Fine." His eyes flashed with something close to defiance before falling, he couldn't look at any of us when he spoke. "Rhys Kelly is my stepbrother."

"Explain." Xavier's bark made me and Dante flinch.

"Our parents married after he was convicted and in prison. I was told who he was and what he did, of course, but there wasn't much I could do at that point but pretend I didn't know." He took a deep breath, steadying himself for what was coming next.

I spoke before he could. "I was talking to the matchmaker at Omega Services about placement and pack for my first heat. I gave her everyone's names. Richie's pulled a flag in the system."

"And they were obligated to inform you," Dante commented.

All eyes moved to him; I could see the knowledge in his gaze as he looked at me. "You know."

He nodded. "I also had a call with the matchmaker. Although, I think mine was a bit different than yours."

"My call was pretty weird," I admitted. "When I said I wanted another omega with me they insisted I have a psych evaluation."

"That explains why my matchmaker told me insanity was contagious." Our laughter filled the silence around us; the men seemed to be in shock from what they were seeing. "She also told me of Richie's familial relationship."

"You knew all this time?" Richie's voice drew all our attention to him.

"What I didn't know was why that made Penelope run from me."

"I wasn't running from you." I rolled over until I was able to wrap myself around him. "I was running from a painful memory. Can we not talk about this right now?"

Dante reached down and pressed a kiss to my forehead. "Our pack is here to provide what you need princess."

"Distract me."

"You heard her boys." They moved from around us at his command. "We need to sit up."

I rolled off him, shimmying up until I was sitting beside him at the top of the bed. Our hands wrapped around each other before I laid my head on his shoulder. He always made me feel safe, something that no one else had been able to do since I left. My eyes moved to the end of the bed, the men were kneeling, their arms clasped behind their backs, heads down as if they were waiting for something. I knew that pose all too well.

"You're so tense." Dante murmured. "Talk to me princess."

"The pose."

It was the only thing I could say. Dante nodded, understanding evident in his next words. "Less formality guys, Penelope doesn't like it."

They took a moment to get more comfortable; when they settled I was stunned by the beauty of the moment. Three powerfully built men kneeling, waiting for the command to please their omegas. Xavier and Evan's eyes were still down, but Richie stared at me; it felt like a challenge. There was something rising up in my chest telling me not to let that stand. The idea of making him submit to me made me wet. I watched as my perfume slammed into him, his eyes widened realizing what it meant.

"This is going to be fun." Richie's voice offended me for some reason.

I opened my mouth to start to correct him, but Dante spoke before I could. "Ask him what he likes."

"I'm a brat." Richie interrupted. "There isn't a thing she could do to me that I wouldn't welcome. And if I don't want it, I have my safe word."

"You should probably have one of those too," Dante whispered in my ear. "Something you would never say in the bedroom. The least sexy thing you can think of."

"Can we use the redlight system? It's just easier."

"Proceed." It felt like he was dismissing me, and I didn't like it.

"Fuck all the way off, asshole," I snapped at him.

He had the audacity to laugh at me. "I'll punish you later, princess. Tonight is about you being in charge."

"I love you."

"I have loved you since the first moment I saw you, don't look so doubtful, I still remember the first words you said to me." Dante traced my bottom lip with his thumb.

"Stop smiling and help me beat Richie up."

We shared a laugh before he continued, "I told you whatever you needed I would provide. I suppose I should have made myself clearer. You are *my omega* just as these are my men. Over time they will become your men as well."

"I won't be her anything." I would have been insulted at the rejection if that voice hadn't belonged to Xavier. He always only wanted Dante and no one but. I loved him all the more for it.

I smiled when I saw the happiness in Dante's eyes at his alpha's statement. "I never expected you to, Xavier. You've always been destined for Dante only."

That made Dante grin even wider. "Now tell them what you want. Evan listens well enough, but as you've seen, Richie is a bit of a brat."

"You bet your ass I am."

My head turned and I could see the smirk on Richie's face. "That's it. You don't get any pussy tonight."

"That's fine. I'll just fuck Dante."

"One week," I said smugly.

"One week, what?" Richie asked.

I shared a look with Dante, shooting him a wink before adding again. "Two weeks."

"No sex for two weeks?"

"I can't speak for Dante or anyone else. But yes, no sex with me for two weeks." I nodded.

"No sex period for two weeks," Dante chimed in.

"That's unfair. You're due to go into heat any day now." There was real desperation in Richie's voice.

I took a breath, thinking about the last heat I had. It had been a while; I was with Cain for about six weeks. Doing quick math in my head, I shook my head. "I haven't been here that long. There's no way."

"What was that, princess?"

"I am too..." I chewed on my bottom lip. "I didn't think I had been here long enough. We certainly haven't spent enough time together..."

"Princess, I need you to take a breath and talk to me."

"I'm going into heat soon. Sooner than I should be." The admission was pulled from me in a desperate gasp.

"It's probably coincidence." Dante sounded sure. "But my heat starts soon too. I can already feel it coming."

Richie looked at us with confusion in his eyes. "How do you know?"

"I know my heat schedule."

I laughed when Dante sounded insulted. "Baby." I pulled his attention to me. "Richie was talking to me. I learned long ago to hide my heats."

Dante changed the subject before it got too heavy. "Okay, so, two weeks isn't unreasonable."

"I have an idea." There was something evil in the way I grinned. "I need tape or something and something to bind him to."

"Princess, we don't use tape, we aren't monsters," Dante laughed.

He climbed off the bed, going to one of the pictures on the wall. Pulling it out enough to reach behind it, he punched in a code. There was a mechanical whirring as wooden shelving moved down from the ceiling. My eyes moved up, noticing the shelving suspended up there for the first time. It was an ingenious system. I spotted a cage built into a table; my mind wondered for a moment what I could do with that.

Dante followed my gaze, smiling when he saw what I was looking at. "Good choice."

"You wouldn't dare," Richie challenged me.

He was too sure of himself, an idea hit me then. "Crawl to me, alpha."

Richie fell to his palms and moved toward me. I would have thought a full-grown man, a mountain of an alpha, wouldn't have had the grace to make crawling look sexy. Richie proved that wrong, he moved like a large cat, as at home on all fours as he was on his feet. Everything about him made me want more.

Chapter 24

Xavier

I may not have cared for Penelope, but I had to admit, she had a way with Richie that I envied. The alpha was wild—nearly feral, always needing a firm hand in and out of the bedroom. I sincerely hoped that she would be able to handle him. Dante would provide her with as much guidance as she needed, but she would need to get her feet under her fast. I was watching the play as Richie pulled a classic brat move and lifted her onto the bench by her waist. He pushed her legs back, burying his face between her thighs. My eyes kept moving back to Dante, where he was seeming to enjoy the show.

His cock was straining against his pants; the growing wet spot made my mouth water. I crossed the room and had Dante by his waist before he could react. Lifting him, I carried my omega the short distance to the bed, muscles flexing as I tossed him onto it. He bounced when he landed, releasing the most adorable giggle. The blush that spread across his face at the feminine gesture made me want to eat him alive. I intended to do just that. Pulling his shorts down, I tossed them over my shoulder as I moved his legs so they were pressed against his chest. His arms moved, holding his legs in place, providing me the access I desired.

That wasn't what I wanted, I wanted to look into his eyes as I made him fall apart. I lay on the bed beneath him; I was so close to what I craved but he wasn't in the right position. My hand slid between his legs, wrapping around his cock. My hand moved up his shaft until my thumb teased his head, making him leak for me. I released him and placed both hands on his thighs to push them open leaving me with a view of my omega. My head dipped, my tongue lashing out to catch the shining pearl sitting there. It was delicious, tasting so much like cinnamon buns that I couldn't hold back the moan that came rumbling from my chest. My lips wrapped around his head, savoring the sweetness of him. My head moved down, my throat relaxing around him until he was buried.

"Fuck, alpha." His hand found a place on the back of my head, holding me against him.

He was leaking sweet liquid straight down my throat. My moan vibrated around him, making his head fall back onto the pillow. My tongue circled his head, lapping at the slit there before working him the rest of the way down my throat. He was just large enough that I could swallow around him, tightening down around his head. His hand tightened in my hair, holding me pressed against him. He fucked my face with little thrusts of his hips.

"Fuck alpha, I'm going to cum." I growled around him, knowing he liked the way it vibrated around his cock. His grip on my hair would've been painful if not for the flood of pleasure I was getting from him as he emptied himself down my throat.

He relaxed in steps beneath me, releasing his hold on my hair, his hand coming to rest on his stomach. Coming up on my knees, I shifted enough to be able to grab the lube out of the nightstand. My free hand slid between Dante's cheeks; opening the bottle, I poured a liberal amount on my fingers and started to work him open. "You want my cock, baby boy?"

"I need it, alpha."

"Such a good boy." I twisted my fingers, aiming upward until he moaned for me. I loved wringing those delicious sounds out of him.

There was movement behind me, the bed dipped, and I felt hands on my chest as I worked Dante open. "You think our omega could take all of us?" Evan's voice in my ear made my cock even harder.

"We could always find out."

"You're wearing too many clothes for that." Evan's hands were already moving, gripping my shirt, and tearing it off me. The shreds landed on either side of me.

"I liked that shirt."

He leaned forward and kissed my throat. "I'll buy you a new one."

"I need…" Dante's voice was echoed by Penelope's from across the room.

"The omegas seem to think you two are taking too long."

"Well, they can damn well use their voices," I snapped.

"If you don't fuck me soon, I will kill you." Penelope snarled into the room.

Dante laughed. "I'll make her the weapon, hurry the fuck up."

Evan was already sliding my shorts down and pushing me forward. My fingers slid from inside Dante as the beta leaned over and wrapped a lubed hand around my cock. I nearly collapsed from the pleasure as he stroked me with infuriating slowness. He moved my cock until I was pushing up against Dante, the head just inside him. Evan disappeared from behind me as I pushed into the omega; his head fell back against the pillows with a sigh of relief. My hips moved in small circles teasing him with each movement.

His legs came up, wrapping around my waist as he pulled me down into a kiss. Our lips met as my thrusts increased until I was slamming him into the mattress, making him bounce with every movement. He was stretched around me, and it wasn't enough for either of us. His hips moved in time with mine, until he was starting to expand around my knot. He was so close to taking all of me. I gave into that insidious thought, pushing forward until my knot popped inside him.

I was standing alone in the kitchen later that night, waiting for the feeling of the house to settle. There was something that wasn't quite right anymore, and I couldn't place my finger on it. The coffee was just starting to brew when Penelope swept into the room trailing my pack's combined scents. It annoyed me that she got everything she wanted, but it was past time that we put this behind us.

"Xavier." She hesitated in the doorway. "I didn't know you were up."

The silence grew thick around us as we both refused to engage. This cold war had been going on long enough and one of us would have to end it. I sighed, opening my lips to speak, but she beat me there. "Can we go back to being friends?"

"Maybe someday." I shook my head. "It took years for me to be able to not outright hate you."

"I know that."

"Do you?" I pressed.

"I know it couldn't have been easy."

"Dante almost died when you left. That wasn't just hard, it was devastating. But that isn't the half of it." I pushed a loc out of my face as I took a few deep breaths to try and keep my anger in check. "I didn't understand what went so wrong for you to have to leave. I always made sure you were safe and welcome, didn't I?"

"You did."

I nodded. "Then why didn't you come and talk to me?"

"I didn't want to make you have to choose."

"What choice?"

She stared at me across the island. "If I'd told you that I couldn't stay in the pack if Richie was part of it, you would have picked me?"

"In a heartbeat." She seemed not to believe me. "Richie was only with us because Dante kind of liked him. Our omega definitely liked you."

"Oh."

"I can't promise I'm always going to be nice to you."

That made her laugh. "When are you ever?"

"But we can work on being friends again." I held my hand out to her. "Let's go back to bed."

Chapter 25

Rhys

I should have been hundreds of miles from here. Anywhere would have been better than standing next to a dispatcher's house. But the woman who answered my call seemed so familiar. I couldn't place where I knew her from at the time. It wasn't her name, though I knew that last name well. Her mother's murder was what put me in prison. No, it was her voice that did it. The only man I shared a cell with had managed to sneak in a cell phone. He had audio recordings of her. His obsession with her was creepy enough that I beat his head in. The second I slid into her passenger seat I knew I had to have her. Nothing would stand in my way; she was mine and there was nothing anyone could do about it.

That led me to the man I was currently staring down. There was nothing particularly memorable about him, just an average white male beta. He wasn't even my normal victim type. This one couldn't have a child even if you gave him illustrated instructions. No, he was at the end of my blade because he was a matchmaker for Omega Services. "Tell me, which one of your colleagues was in charge of Penelope Shannon's matching."

"I remember her, tight little ass she had on her."

Rage made me slam the blade into his stomach, twisting before removing it. “You were her matchmaker, weren’t you?”

“Yes.”

“Good. Now I advise you to tell me the truth and I will make this easy on you.” I brought the blade up to the light, watching the blood sparkle as the glow reflected along its length. “Or you could lie to me, and I could have some fun.”

“I...I won’t lie to you.”

I sincerely hoped he’d lie to me. The monster inside me was screaming to let loose. I was inclined to let it have its fun. “Now tell me, what pack did you match Penelope with?”

“She was matched with the best pack we had available. Penelope...” I reacted on instinct, slamming the blade down and pinning his hand to the table. His scream was delicious, making my heart pound with excitement at the thought of inflicting more pain on him. My cock ached from it. Penelope would pay for that later. “I didn’t fucking lie.”

“Don’t say her fucking name.”

My growl made him flinch, the movement making blood pour from the wound. “I matched her with the best pack. I promise that.”

“You mean the pack that could put the most money in your pocket for an omega’s first heat.” I pulled the blade from his hand and slammed it into his shoulder with one movement. “I know you lied to me, so we do this the hard way.”

I left the blade in his shoulder and turned to my table. Before, when I killed, it was always methodical, never wanting to get caught. Not having anything to lose was liberating. I was going to take my time with the beta, explore a little. I started with the filet knife; the blade seemed sharp enough to do what I wanted it to. Smiling when I turned around, I was suddenly very glad I had remembered to tie the beta to the chair. He was staring at me with wide, terrified eyes. Coming back to where I had been sitting, I grabbed ahold of his intact hand. My eyes moved up to his, taking in the panic as he realized he had no way out.

"I won't lie to you and say this isn't going to hurt." I didn't wait for his response.

Lining the blade up with the meat of his arm, I started to cut into him. Angling the knife away from me, I caught the skin and pulled it back as I moved. Blood dripped from the wound as I removed the skin in one solid piece. He was hysterical, telling me everything he knew by the time I sliced through that last bit of tissue connecting the skin to his arm. Problem was, I wasn't done with him. I was just debating what to do when I heard the door open.

Chapter 26

Penelope

Sneaking out was so much easier when everyone in the house had been fucked to sleep. There was nothing stopping me from going after my real target. Unfortunately, I hadn't been able to get my new axe from Dante just yet. He didn't even know I was the one he was making them for. Leaving the property was liberating, I would be taking a large part of myself back from the people who stole it from me. If Calliope could do it, so could I. It had taken me a while to track down the matchmaker; I would make him talk and kill my way through the network that sold me—one pack at a time if necessary.

I would never forget the man's face. Why they had given me a male matchmaker was beyond me, but they had. The pack options he had presented me with were lackluster to say the least. I suspected he had me earmarked for sale from the moment my name passed his desk. Yet here I was, free, and getting ready to kick in his front door, axe in hand. I stopped just before I kicked and tried the handle. When the knob turned, I pushed the door slowly open. The house was quiet, eerily so. My head turned to the right and I was treated to the sight of my matchmaker tied to a chair. My pulse started to quicken as I was hit with the scent of soured laundry.

Blood was collecting on the floor beneath the man. From how much he was losing he didn't have much longer to live. I moved down the hallway, toward that room, until a noise from beyond the doorway made me stop. I froze in place, preparing myself for whatever was coming. Taking a deep breath, I charged into the room. I was not prepared for the sight that met me. Rhys was standing in the corner with all the kitchen knives laid out in front of him on the table. Each of them was dripping blood onto the floor letting me know they had all been used. My eyes moved to the alpha standing beside the table, allowing me to take him in for the first time.

He was much taller than me, taller even than Bradley, who was the largest of Dante's pack. I couldn't imagine a world where he wouldn't have to duck through doorways. He emphasized the size difference by coming toward me. Looking up at him, I felt truly tiny . With him in my space I could smell his petrichor scent, it made me want to wrap myself around his bulk. My hand moved, wanting to see if he was as soft as he looked. That was yet another way he was so different from my men. They were all muscles and hard lines; Rhys just looked soft and cuddly. His hand came out, catching my wrist and pulling me against his chest. He was just as soft as he looked, making me moan from the feeling.

"You like when I take charge, don't you, angel?" God this man was smooth.

I pushed back against him; I couldn't be in his arms. Not when I should be sinking my axe into his chest. He killed my mother, killed her pack—stole my childhood from me. There was no reason I should want this alpha with his grey hair and piercing hazel eyes. "I don't like anything about you."

"Don't lie to me. I can smell how wet you are."

"It's not for you."

The lie left my lips so fast I didn't even take time to consider what that meant. "So... you get off on watching someone die?"

"That's not what I meant and you know it."

There was a sound from the beta tied to the chair. He was still bleeding, but it was slowing to a worrying rate. He was going to die before I could get the answers I needed from him. I couldn't have that. Moving across the room, I grabbed a towel and pressed it to the worst of the wounds. My free hand snapped forward, slamming into the side of his face. His eyes flew open at the instant pain, panic in his eyes. "Just let me die." He was broken, and I didn't feel even an ounce of pity for him.

"Not until you tell me everything," I hissed.

He was losing consciousness and there was nothing I could do to stop it. "You might as well let him die. I already have all your answers."

My head popped up; my eyes locked on Rhys' when he said that. "What are you doing here?"

I was already moving away from the beta, stepping back toward Rhys before hesitating. The axe was still in my hand. I came here to start my journey, determined to end this beta. I still wanted to stay on that path. Raising the axe was the easy part, bringing it down was much harder than I expected. My arms ached from holding it in the air. I felt Rhys come up behind me, his hands finding mine on the handle. His muscles flexed as he brought the axe down on the beta's head. He fell to the side and his last breath rattled from him as I watched.

"How do you feel?" Rhys asked as he stepped back enough for me to be able to turn in his arms.

"Like I started something I won't be able to stop."

"That's how it felt for me. That, and freedom." He stepped back, pulling the axe from my hand as he spun me in place. "Like I'd finally shed the shackles that polite society tried to force on me. People like us aren't meant to be confined by the accepted rules of society. We are the things society fears."

My hands found my hips as I stared at the alpha. "You're so sure that I am anything like you."

"I know you are. You aren't as good at controlling your perfume as you think you are." He boxed me in with his arms, spinning us until my back was to the wall. I was pinned, my eyes scanned for a way out, my heart pounding. His hand slid inside my pants, two fingers finding my heat, pushing them inside. I fought not to moan for him. “There are only two reasons you would be this soaked right now.”

His arm twisted, fingers moving as he slid them along my g-spot. My walls tightened around him, nearly making my knees buckle. “There is nothing you can say that would make me want you.”

“Oh, really?” His thumb teased my clit as he spoke. “So, you don’t want me to know you were wet the moment you saw me. You really don’t want me to know that murdering the beta made you soaked.”

“I...” My words were cut off as his thumb triggered an orgasm that made my legs shake beneath me. My hands came up, catching his shoulders instinctively. “Fuck you,” I ground out through clenched teeth.

“That was an orgasm if I’ve ever seen one.”

His thumb was already moving, his fingers pumping inside me, steadily pushing me toward a second one. “You can try and claim me all you want. It’s—” The orgasm crested as I moaned out the last words, “not going to work.”

“Seems to be working just fine.” He was steadily pushing me toward a third orgasm. I was riding the edge when he spoke again. “Admit you want me, and I’ll tell you what I learned.”

I fought all I could to not say what I knew deep in my heart. “Fine, I fucking want you. That doesn’t mean I want to fuck you.”

“Cheeky little omega.”

“Now tell me.”

He pushed me over the edge, my orgasm nearly sending me crashing to the ground. Pulling his fingers from me, I whined at the loss of them. I didn’t get another sound out before I was in the air, he had a firm grip on my ass as he moved until I was sitting against the wall. Bracing us with one hand, he used the other to line his cock up. His head was just inside me when my eyes flew open.

My arm snapped back, slamming forward to send his head to the side. His hips moved until he was buried inside me. “You’re going to pay for that.”

“Fuck all the way off.” Try as I might, I couldn’t stop myself from wrapping my arms around his neck. My ankles finding their place on his hips as I rode him for all he was worth.

His hand slid between us, finding my clit. His teasing sent me crashing over the edge, spiraling straight into a bone- melting orgasm. I collapsed against him, the only thing keeping me in the air was his grip on my ass. As he slammed into me, I was waiting for the moment he was going to knot me. I had a sinking feeling in my gut that when he did, I was going to lose myself in this man. Distancing myself from what was happening wasn’t an option, I needed every chance I had to try and get away from him.

My chance came when he shifted me so I was on the floor. Metal glinting in the light drew my attention; my axe was sitting there, within reach. I studied Rhys, waiting for him to make the wrong move. His eyes closed. Reaching for the axe I was just able to grab the bottom of the handle. Praying he didn’t hear the scraping of the metal, I worked my hand up until I could catch the grip. I swung it without looking, hoping I managed to connect.

That hope was dashed when his hand closed around mine. “You’ve got some fight in you, that’s good.”

My breath rushed out when he pulled out of me. The relief was short- lived when I felt his hands on the back of my thighs, pushing them back so they rested against my chest. Pushing against that pressure did no good, he was much stronger than me, making it impossible to get out of this. Cold metal pressed against me, making me squirm; the feeling of the base stretching me, filling me with a chill I couldn’t escape. I was tense, shaking from the invasion.

“That’s not comfortable.” I was shifting around, trying to find a position I could bear. My brain was struggling to catch up with what was happening to me. I couldn’t get a grip on anything. Maybe this was what shock felt like, I wasn’t entirely sure. As he worked the handle in and out of me, making me gush, I didn't even really feel the orgasms anymore. I was so detached from the situation that I just submitted. "Where did that fight from earlier go?"

Sometime while I was lost in my head he had moved me, my leg was bent to the side so he could slide in behind me. "Just let me go."

"I'll make you a deal." He twisted the axe just right, making me moan and tighten down around the metal. His hand snaked around me, teasing my clit until I lost myself to the pleasure.

I came alive like a woman possessed, fucking myself on the handle until I was gushing around it. My slick coated the ground, making my scent thicker in the air. I knew the moment he lost all that careful control he had. His arm flexed, pulling the metal from me and tossing the weapon across the room. His cock was buried inside me before I could react, the curve of it stroking along my g-spot until I tightened down around him. It was almost painful as I struggled to push him from me. His firm grip held me in place, the swell of his knot just starting to stretch me around him. My vision swam as he pushed into me, the pain making my vision start to black out. I let out the breath I had been holding when he popped inside me.

"You feel so good squeezing my cock like that," He groaned as I felt him pumping inside me. "You're mine now."

I hated the finality in his voice. "Never."

"We'll see about that."

I felt his breath on the back of my neck as he moved just enough to press a gentle kiss there. My head tilted before I could stop myself. He filled that space, nipping at my throat. I moaned for him as he lapped at my throat. Kissing his way to the spot he had chosen, I tensed when he nipped there. There was a brief moment of pain when he broke the skin before I was lost to the feeling. The bond settled into place quickly, sending pleasure through me. I couldn't tell if it was mine or his. Pushing against the settling bond, I was suddenly able to feel what he did.

It was mostly satisfaction, he had finally claimed me. The feeling of him filling me made me spasm around him, flooding me with happiness. I knew that came from him. He released that bit of flesh he had held in his teeth, lapping at the wound. He displayed a level of care I didn't think he was capable of. Studying what he was feeling even more closely, I discovered there was a level of protectiveness he felt toward me. For some strange reason, that allowed me to relax into his hold, letting the feeling of him taking care of me lull me to sleep.

Chapter 27

Xavier

Penelope was already gone when we woke up. Going to the kitchen, I started coffee and began making breakfast. I was studying the ingredients in the fridge when I heard someone come into the room. Turning, I spotted Evan. He crossed the room and pressed a kiss to my cheek. "Morning."

I could tell he was half asleep as he cleaned the gunk from his eyes. "Morning. Bacon or sausage?"

"Bacon."

"Good." I grabbed the eggs, bacon, and mayo from the fridge and went to the stove.

The smell of bacon cooking was just starting to fill the air when the front door opened. Penelope stumbled through, looking as if she had been hit by a bus. Her hair was all over the place, bags beneath her eyes gave the look that she had been crying. She refused to look at either of us. "Are you okay?" My voice boomed into the silence.

"I'm fine." Her voice was too small for my liking, her hand coming up to wrap a strand of her hair around her finger.

"You are clearly not fine. Come take a seat." My head nodded, indicating the chair at the bar. "Evan, make the woman some coffee."

The beta jumped to do as I asked, setting a steaming mug in front of her as she slid into the seat. Her hand found her hair again, taking a lock and twisting it almost absentmindedly. "It's really nothing, I'm okay."

"You have the worst habit of playing with your hair when you lie. You should really work on that."

Whatever she was about to say next was cut off by Bradley and Dante sweeping into the kitchen. Dante slid by me in an effort to make coffee. I caught him before he managed it, spinning him around and pulling him into a deep kiss. His hands slid around my waist as he held me close. Dante broke the kiss, his voice breathless. "Good morning."

My omega made his coffee, sliding into place next to Penelope at the bar. I watched as Dante eyed her with suspicion in his eyes. "What's wrong?"

"Nothing."

"We really need to work on your ability to lie." There was something in his voice that made me pause at the stove. "Now tell me what happened."

The command in Dante's voice was not to be ignored. Penelope responded to it, her voice tentative as she spoke, "I went out last night. There was something I had to do."

"Does that something have to do with why you're covered in blood?" She chewed on her lip as if debating how much she wanted to admit to. "You know who my twin is. There's no need to lie."

Dante's urging was all it took. "I wanted to kill the matchmaker that set me up with the pack that sold me."

"And did you find him?"

My eyes moved to Bradley where he was frozen, standing in front of the coffee pot. I could see the tension in his back. His hands were resting on the counter, his grip so tight his knuckles were white. "I did." Penelope wouldn't look at anyone when she answered.

"And I assume he is no longer with us." Dante's gaze bore into her.

"That's right."

"Did you...?" Bradley spoke for the first time. He was already moving, coming around the island to pull Penelope into his arms. "Did you kill him?"

"I struck the final blow." She took a breath before adding the next part. "Rhys was there already. He tortured the matchmaker before I could get there."

"Excuse the fuck out of me?!" All our heads turned as Richie walked into the room.

Penelope pulled out of Bradley's arms and went to the other alpha. There was desperation in her voice when she spoke, "I needed to do something; he set me up to be sold."

"I could give two shits about the man you killed. He had it coming." He confirmed he heard the whole conversation. "Rhys was there..."

"About that..."

His hands were already moving, scanning her for injuries as he moved her clothing around to see what he could find. He took a firm grip on her chin and moved her head to the side. "I'm going to kill him." We could all feel the rage vibrating off Richie.

The front door slammed open as the largest man I had ever seen walked in. He towered over the rest of us, his bulk filling the space. Rhys Kelly was standing in my kitchen. "I would suggest you unhand my omega and stop questioning her."

"She had no say in you marking her." Richie's growl spread through the room.

"Little murderess, tell my stepbrother what you were doing when I marked you."

"Coming around your cock." I wasn't in the least bit surprised; she had been attracted to bad boys since childhood.

"And what exactly was it that made me lose control and sink my teeth into that delicate throat?"

"Some combination of taking and using me as you wished, no matter what I had to say about it." Growls erupted around the room at that. My own adding to the building rumble. "It might have also had something to do with my slick making my scent so thick you could see it in the air around us."

"Good girl." Rhys's voice made Penelope shiver in Richie's arms. "Come here, little murderess."

Penelope went to him, his arm sliding across her shoulders as he pulled her against his side. She looked comfortable but unsure of herself. My eyes scanned the room, hoping that no one did anything stupid. That was when I noticed that Dante had slipped from the room at some point. Just then, a whine spilled from the nest, breaking the tension. My spine snapped straight, my head turning on instinct. I knew Dante whining meant his heat was coming. Setting the spatula on the counter, as I headed toward the nest, I was stopped by Bradley's hand on my arm. "You're alpha."

"No shit." I grumbled at him.

"You misunderstand. Me and Evan have Dante for now. You need to deal with this." I nodded. He studied my face for a moment before leaving me to face the escaped serial killer in my house.

Crossing my arms across my chest, I faced the man down. "What exactly do you want, Rhys?"

"I'd like to know the same thing." Richie's voice was the last thing I wanted to hear at that moment.

"I wasn't talking to you," I snapped at my pack mate. Turning back to Rhys, I asked my question again. "What do you want here, Rhys?"

"I only long to be around my sweet little murderess. So long as no one," he stared at Richie pointedly, "tries to keep her from me, there shouldn't be a problem."

"And Dante?"

"I've never killed an omega in my life. I don't plan on starting now."

I uncrossed my arms and held one of my hands out to the older alpha. "Welcome to the pack, I guess. We can get everything worked out later."

I left them standing there with Richie while I went to be with my omega.

Chapter 28

Bradley

Dante and Penelope had been having heat spikes for the last week, and I couldn't figure out the problem I was having at the moment. I needed to figure it out before their heats hit. Reaching out to Ayden was the only option I had. Loathe as I was to involve him, I needed his expertise. I was just reaching for my phone when Richie swept into the room. "I have to tell someone, and I know you won't say anything."

"Won't say anything about what?"

"I know where Amani is."

That made me spin in the chair until I was staring at him. "Run that by me again. Slowly."

"Xavier's sister. Amani. I know where she is."

"And you're telling me and not him, why?"

He ran his hand through his hair in a nervous motion. "You know that shelter we send all the omegas we rescue to?"

I sighed, he was making me fish, I hated it when he did that. "And that has to do with Amani how?"

"She owns it."

He was so sure of himself it was making me question what I knew. "There's no way. I did the research before we started using the shelter, Dorian owns it."

"Either way, she's there." He shrugged, turning to leave the room.

"Oh no you don't." I moved as quickly as I could, grabbing his arm as I passed, leading him out into the living room. "We're going to visit this shelter and have a talk with Dorian." We walked close to each other heading to the garage.

Richie and I were out, in the car, and headed toward the warehouse that held the shelter moments later. The drive took less time than it should have considering I was driving like a bat out of hell. "I'd like to make it back to my omega in one piece."

"You're going to be very lucky if you make it back to her at all."

"Don't threaten me." His snarl would have been cute if it very well may not have been his last.

"It's not me that's a threat to you." I ignored the irritated sound he released as I pulled into the parking lot for the shelter. "I can't speak for what our alpha will do when he finds out you knew where his sister was."

I didn't give him a chance to respond as I exited the car and rushed to the front door. The handle was turning in my hand before Richie caught up with me. Dorian's eyes caught mine as soon as I swept into the building. "Bradley, I didn't know–"

"Where is she?"

"I am sure I don't know who you are talking about." He was shooting panicked glances toward a room behind the desk.

"I know Amani is here. Now you can tell me where I can find her so we can talk, or I can get her brother on the phone and you can answer to him."

He hesitated long enough for me to start to move around the desk, toward the office door behind it. "You can't go in there."

"I would suggest you get your hand off me before I remove it from your body." The threat flew from my lips without thought.

My growl rose to match his, the tension between us rising until it was at a nearly deadly level. I tensed, ready to do anything necessary to get to Amani. She had to be in this office, there was no question about it. His eyes fell from mine, his hand releasing my arm, allowing me to push into the office. I smiled as soon as I saw her sitting there.

"Richie told you." There was the confidence I remembered.

"What did you expect? Richie was never all that good at keeping secrets." I shrugged. "It's good to see you're okay."

"I'm sorry I left the way I did."

The way her eyes fell when she spoke made my stomach twist. She shouldn't be afraid of me, she shouldn't be afraid of anyone. "You don't owe me anything."

"Still, I should have said something to someone."

"It wouldn't have worked if you had."

She rewarded me with one of her megawatt smiles. "You're right there."

"I don't have a right to ask you what happened and why, but can I ask how you are?"

She sighed, leaning back in the chair before motioning for me and Richie to take seats across from her. "Life hasn't been easy." I could hear the weight in her voice as she spoke. "I've had to do things to survive, to protect my shelter." She shook her head. "I'm fine now."

"I'm glad to hear that. May I ask if you found your pack yet?"

"That's complicated." She was smiling as she said it, but I knew she was lying, there was a combination of scents here that gave it away. "Dorian has been taking care of me just fine."

My phone started ringing before I could ask the next question. Pulling it from my pocket, I saw it was Xavier calling. "It's your brother."

She took a deep breath before nodding. "Put it on speaker."

Answering the phone, my voice shook as I spoke. "Hello."

"Why do you sound so nervous?" Xavier's booming voice filled the room, distorted as it was coming from the speaker.

"I just needed to stop by the shelter and deal with something."

"Anything I should be aware of?" He was so calm, and I hated knowing I was lying to him.

Amani reached over and took the phone from my hand. "I don't know."

"Who was that?"

"You don't recognize your sister's voice?" Her laugh made a smile cross my face. "I know it's been five years, but I haven't changed that much."

"Bradley, you had better not be fucking with me."

The hope in his voice made me want to reach over and snatch the phone from her. "Why don't you show up and find out." She hung up as he started to swear. She was all smiles.

Chapter 29

Xavier

Whoever the woman on the phone was, she sure as fuck sounded a lot like my baby sister. I debated calling our parents, but if it were Amani, she wouldn't want me to tell them. Not now at least. Maybe not ever. I was driving on autopilot, trying to figure out what happened. Pulling into the parking lot, I parked next to Bradley's Pilot. I needed a moment to gather myself before I went inside.

"Are you okay, alpha?" Dante's voice from the passenger seat made me jump.

"I'm fine, I just need a minute."

"You're far from fine." He reached across the cab and placed a hand on my arm. "But it's okay, I'm here."

Taking a deep breath, I reached over and caressed his cheek. "I know you are, baby boy."

Getting out, I came around to where Dante was waiting for me to open the door for him. I did so and he got out, his arm wrapping around my elbow as I guided him inside. I hated knowing he was in such a place, but I also hated knowing my sister was here. When I helped her run, I wouldn't have expected her to completely disappear from me. But that was exactly what she had done.

Pushing inside, desperation filled the air, making it nearly impossible to discern one scent from all the others. I scanned the lobby, hoping to be able to find her in the crowd of omegas. I half hoped not to find her in that group, half hoped Bradley was wrong. To find her here would mean she had been…I wouldn't finish that thought, it was too much.

"Over here." Bradley's voice called to me from behind the desk.

I headed there, sweeping past the other alpha, pushing my omega ahead of me. Sure, Dante was safe, but I pulled Bradley behind me until I heard the click of the door as he closed it. My eyes moved, hovering over every person in the room before stopping at the woman behind the large desk there. "You're actually here."

"You seriously thought your pack was lying to you?" She scoffed.

"I can't trust any of them, let alone Richie." I snapped at the other alphas. "Now tell me everything."

"There isn't much to tell. Dorian and I ended up together not long after I left, and we've been pretty much inseparable since."

"There's something you aren't telling me."

I watched her thought process before she smiled. "It might be better if I show you."

She stood, moving to the file cabinet, and pulling on it. When it swung open, it revealed a set of stairs. We followed her down until we were in a large living room. I couldn't help my curiosity as I scanned the room, looking for any indication she had a pack. The more I looked, the more I saw the touches. There was a blanket spread across the back of the couch where Amani took a seat; it was a very rustic touch, something neither her nor Dorian would like. In the kitchen there were five coffee mugs sitting on the counter.

"So, you have a pack now?" I was teasing her. "I thought you didn't want one of those."

"I didn't, I don't. But things change."

"What things?" I pressed.

That question was answered by a tiny red-headed omega and a large alpha coming out of what I assumed was the nest. "Amani." The redhead went to her, climbing onto her lap and pressing her nose against Amani's throat.

"You have a pack." It was a statement, but she knew I was expecting an answer.

"It's a recent development," she admitted. "Really recent. She'll probably be going into heat soon."

"On that note," Dante pulled me to my feet. "I have an omega of my own at home to take care of."

"You can meet your niece next time." Amani called after us.

Dante flat out refused to let me go back in there.

Chapter 30

Penelope

Rhys was bound and determined to get on my last nerve. There wasn't a second that he wasn't glued to my side. It was the most infuriating thing about him. Not that any part of this was comfortable, but he could have at least given me some breathing room. As it was, we were in the basement nest while Evan waited at the door to take me to work.

"I have work. I need to go." I stepped away from his grasp, going to the dresser and pulling out my uniform. "Don't you have things you could be doing while I'm there?"

"I don't have anything I need to do but keep my omega safe."

Rage slid through me, there was only so much I could take. "I need space god damn it. I can't spend every second of every day glued to you. That just isn't going to work."

"You don't even want me here."

"You're fucking right I don't want you here, I don't want anything to do with you!" My hands balled into fists at my side. "I told you that before you marked me."

“And I told you that you are mine. I don’t particularly care about whether you want me or not. I’m here, deal with it.”

“You’re such a fucking asshole.”

“But I’m your asshole.” He had the audacity to wink at me. “And don’t think I can’t tell that our fighting turns you on. If I came over there I’d find you soaked, wouldn’t I?”

“Go to hell!”

“I’ve spent nearly fifty years there.” His voice held just a thread of emotion—that was interesting. “Every second without you is hell.”

I was stunned for a moment. There was nothing about him that made me think he felt anything, let alone as profoundly as that. “You don’t even know me.” All of the bravado disappeared.

“I may not have grown up with you like the other members of your pack, but I know parts of you that they never will.” He stood, coming over until I was looking up at him. “I see the things they don’t. How you chew on your fingernails when you’re stressed out.” He pulled my hand up to his lips and kissed the tips of my fingers. “The way your eyes light up when you see torture and pain. How comfortable you are in my world of death. Even your day job places you right in the center of crime. You love it. The excitement turns you on and makes you feel like you have control over your life. That’s something you never really had. Part of that is my fault.” I started to speak, but he continued. “The rest I can’t speak for. I don’t regret killing your mother or her pack, don’t think for one second I do.”

“Why did you...?”

“Kill her?” he finished for me. When I nodded, he sighed. “You know what I was convicted of. Nearly everyone does. My M.O. and victim type are public. I told you weeks ago what happened, but it makes me wonder why you don’t believe me.”

“I know the facts...” I searched for the words. “You say I’m yours.”

"You are." His growl made a smile start to crest across my face. Maybe I could make something out of that.

"*You* say I am. Consent is a thing, though you seem to have forgotten that."

He looked very smug as he replied, "Your body knows who it belongs to; your mind just hasn't caught up yet."

"There may come a day when I belong to you, but that isn't today." I brushed past him, pressing a kiss to Evan's cheek as I passed. "Let's get going."

Somehow, I made it to work without any more problems. I didn't expect it to be the last I saw of Rhys, but I was able to focus on work. The first few calls were routine, but the one I was on now was anything but. The woman on the phone was trying to escape someone who was following her. "He's still behind me."

"Take a breath." Coaching her through her panic was a simple thing to do. "I need you to take a left and there should be an officer close to that corner."

I could hear the wheels spinning as she took the turn too quickly. "The cop just lit him up. He's running."

"Let him go." She hung up before I could finish that thought.

I spent the next hour coordinating the chase before I was able to disconnect. Logging out of my computer, I grabbed my cellphone and headed to the break room. Opening the phone, I sent a mass text to my pack letting them know I was okay. Pulling up a search engine, I typed in Rhys' name and scanned the headlines. There were reports about his last murder, the one I had taken the call for. Nothing there about the matchmaker disappearing. That was unusual, but not unexpected. Pulling up the untraceable browser Cain installed on all my devices, I started to search for the pack that tried to sell me. *Tried* because I managed to get away before they could.

Not that it helped matters, the pack that had taken me in was worse, keeping me alive as little better than a live-in maid; groups of men took turns using me. My hands shook as I typed names I remembered into the search bar. Each one led me deeper down a rabbit hole that I hated even existed. There was a whole web of these perverted fuckers out there. All I could think of was how good it would feel to see their blood collecting on the floor. My axe in their skulls, Rhys fucking me next to their bodies.

I tried to imagine a world where I killed and Rhys wasn't there, but when I did, all I could feel was this ache in my chest. There was no reason for me to feel this way, but I did. He had managed to worm his way beneath my skin, and I wasn't too sure I wanted him gone. Fighting with him made my blood boil, but all I could imagine was fucking him after. The thought of killing without him made me want to give up on life. My heart started to ache in my chest at the thought of him not being there. As the panic slammed into me, my phone started to ring.

No caller ID, that made my hand start to shake. "Hello?"

"Little murderess, I can feel your sorrow, tell me what's bothering you." The moment I heard Rhys' voice, all the tension leaked from my body.

"How did you get my number?"

He laughed at the annoyance in my voice. "I know everything about you."

Chapter 31

Richie

There was only so much I could take, especially sitting across from my stepbrother and the man who raped and forcibly marked my omega. It was taking everything in me not to reach over and snap the bastard's neck. I couldn't stop the feeling that everything was spiraling out of control. Bradley wasn't our alpha anymore, he rolled over and let Xavier take it from him. Dante was drifting further and further from me; I could feel the lack of him so acutely it was a persistent ache in my chest.

"God damn it," I growled.

Rhys looked so smug. "Care to share with the room?"

Tension filled me as I started to speak. "Penelope left because of us."

"Explain."

"We all grew up together." I felt like I was letting him into something he had no right to, but this was the only way forward I saw. "Dante and Penelope, the whole pack always thought we would be one of the rare ones that had two omegas."

"What happened?"

"You did," I snapped.

"I find it hard to believe a murder I committed over twenty years ago fucked up your perfect little suburban dream."

"You're right. Blaming you isn't fair." My head fell forward. "I lied to them all. They didn't know anything about our connection. Penelope didn't know until she called the matchmaker."

"They ran your name and found the link."

"They did. And she ran from me."

"You're a bastard, you know that?" He was pissed, I could see as much from the way his hands fisted at his sides. "You don't have any idea what happened to her after she left you."

"I don't." That felt like a confession.

"She was sold. But then that pack traded her. She was swapped around the whole time, used as the alphas' fuck toy. She was exploited and beaten, and only when she knew she was going to be forcibly marked and impregnated did she call her brother. Not you, not fucking Dante. Her god damn brother. This whole pack failed her in so many ways. If I had a say, you all would bleed out while I fucked her on your corpses."

"You do realize you did all the same things to her."

That made him laugh. "And I would do it again. She will come around. There's a difference between what they did to her and what I am doing. Everything I take from her I will use to rebuild her into the version of herself she won't be afraid to look in the eye."

"You don't have to break someone for them to love you."

"You and I see very different versions of the same woman." I started to speak but he continued. "You see the sweet omega you grew up with. The woman who needs love and affection. I see that side of her too, but I also know she has a darkness inside her that is the perfect match for the one that lives inside me. She loves the feeling of blood on her hands, loves to watch wicked people bleed out beneath her. She loves to be taken, owned, and told exactly what she needs. I see the woman behind that strong mask she wears all the time, the one that has to be forced to let someone like me in. I am exactly what she needs, what she has always needed to make this work."

"What's that?"

"I'm the motherfucker that will take out anyone that even looks at her the wrong way. I'm the man that will push her so far past her limits, until all that's left is a raw version of who she is. I'm also the man that will revel in building her into the woman she dreams to be. Whether that involves you and your pack is yet to be seen."

"That's up to her," I retorted.

His sneer as I got up to leave the room was followed by him barking, "That's right."

That was all it took for me to launch a fist into the drywall. Instant regret filled me when I realized I needed to fix that before the omegas got home. Xavier would kill me if either of them were distressed. Heading to the garage, I pulled out the putty and the mesh tape to fix it. Grabbing the razor knife, I set to cutting out the damage and patching the hole. I was so focused on what I was doing that I missed Rhys coming up behind me. "You know, if you line the tape with the putty, it will adhere better."

"You sound like you've done this a lot."

He sighed. "My dad, well, our dad, I guess, was always a violent man. When my mother died, he went to anger management."

"Is that why you're so fucked up?"

"He wasn't abusive by any means, but he did hate omegas. I think it had something to do with him being a beta." He placed a hand on my shoulder. "That's certainly not something he passed on."

"I don't believe that for one moment."

He sighed. "I don't expect you to." He turned, leaving me alone in the house.

My mind fell back to the day I met Penelope.

Coming around the corner of the middle school, I could just make out the sound of someone crying. That sound tugged at something inside me I didn't have a name for. I followed that sound until I spotted her. Coming up beside her I took a seat, pushing her hair out of her face. "Why are you crying, sweetheart?"

"Only my daddy calls me that." Her sniffling made my heart ache.

"Okay, what do you want me to call you?"

She looked up at me, her eyes glistening with unshed tears. "I don't know. No one really talks to me unless they're making fun of me."

"Who makes fun of you?"

She looked over her shoulder at Dante and his group of friends. "The older boys."

"Does Dante or his sister ever say anything?"

"No, they never talk to me." She wiped her eyes before she looked up at me. "Why are you being nice to me?"

"Someone needs to be."

She smiled at me. "I like you."

"I like you too, sweetheart." Standing, I moved away from her, brushing my hand over her shoulder as I passed.

Approaching Dante and his group, I could already see a small pack forming around him. The older boys she was talking about were Xavier and Bradley. There was nothing standing in the way. Dante saw me coming and asked, "Richie." He was smiling as he spoke. "Can I help you with something?"

I nodded. "You know I like you, right?"

"You've made that abundantly clear." Xavier came up behind Dante; I was sure he would be the alpha to Dante's omega.

Dante moved from in front of Xavier and came to me, wrapping his arms around my chest. "I know you like me; I like you too. You're going to be pack."

"We don't know that yet." I nodded at the idea. "Your friends have been mean to someone who matters to me."

"Do you like this someone?"

I smiled. "I think I might."

"Then I'll make sure they're nice to her." Dante released me and went back to Xavier, pulling him back into the group.

I was broken from the memory by the front door opening. I could hear Dante coming in, babbling about something I couldn't quite bring myself to think about. I had long since moved from repairing the wall, and started cooking dinner. I needed something to fill my time, and Dante always loved my cooking. I was half convinced it was the reason he added me to his pack. A smile bloomed on my face as the omega came into the room.

He was devastatingly handsome in an almost effeminate way. It made him all the sexier. He crossed the room and took a seat across the bar from where I was cooking. I kept waiting for him to say something, but there was nothing but heavy silence. When I couldn't take it anymore I finally looked up at him. "I've really made a mess of things, haven't I?"

"A little."

"Is there any saving our pack?"

He stood, coming around. I had to move so he could come to me, my arms were open, and he filled that space much like he did all those years ago. "We aren't in danger of falling apart as a pack unless you let it happen."

"How do I fix this?"

"Stop being so uptight all the time." Dante pulled away and went to Xavier as he walked into the kitchen. "Not everything goes as planned. Just let things happen."

I finished cooking dinner and we ate. We were cuddling on the couch when Dante started to drip sweat. His hands moved as he started to strip, each inch of revealed skin making the air fill with his scent. "Is this a spike?"

"I think so."

Whatever it was didn't matter. I was moving before he finished stripping, my pants falling to the ground as I leaned down to lift him. Moving with a sureness I certainly didn't feel, I carried him up to the nest. I lowered him to the bed and pulled his hips down until he was lying against the end of the bed. Pushing his legs back, I buried my face between his ass cheeks. My tongue lashed out, catching his hole, and lapping my way up his balls. My free hand wrapped around his cock until I was able to wrap my lips around the head. His hand came down to wrap around my hair, forcing me down on him until I was gagging around him. My cock throbbed, aching to fill my omega.

"Such a good boy." Dante's voice made me crave the praise. "Suck your omega's cock."

My hand moved until I was able to slide two fingers between my lips beside his cock. I teased his head with the tips of them until they were wet. I slid them down until I could tease his ass with them. Pushing them inside him I could taste the sweetness of his slick filling my lips. I felt the bed move as Xavier climbed on. His cock was hard and hanging in front of Dante's face. The omega leaned over and wrapped his lips around Xavier's cock. He moaned, sending a shiver up the alpha's spine.

My fingers curved, teasing his prostate until he was squirming. He was soaked for me, and I loved every second of it. Pulling back, I came to my feet, my hand wrapping around my cock as I lined it up with him. My fingers slid out as I started to push inside him. "You ready for my cock, little omega?"

"Please, alpha." His begging was the sexiest thing I'd heard in a long time.

My hips pushed forward, filling him until my knot started to stretch him. His moan made me throb, the feeling of him tightening around me nearly too much. It took everything in me not to slam the rest of the way forward and fill him. I pistoned myself into him, teasing his prostate with my head. "You feel so good squeezing my cock."

His orgasm flooded him, making my cock slide against him in the most delicious way. I was struggling against my instincts to slam all the way home. The pull of his warmth around my knot making me more feral by the moment. My hips slammed home at a punishing pace, working two more orgasms out of him. His cock leaked, his scent making the air thick.

"Please, alpha." His begging was everything in that moment.

"Tell me what you need, little omega."

"Knot me, alpha." He sounded desperate for it.

Dante

The feeling of Richie stretching me around his knot sent me over the edge into another orgasm. I loved every second of his brutal fucking. He always gave me exactly what I needed. The delicious pain of stretching around him was perfect. He was finally seated, making me tighten around him. Flexing my muscles, he lost control, his cock throbbing inside me. It was like a sweet balm, calming my heat with delicious pleasure.

"Alpha." My voice made Richie look up at me. "I need your mark."

His growl made me speed up my movements, his knot throbbing inside me. He was so close to a second orgasm, and I needed his mark before I pushed him over that edge. Tossing my head to the side, I made sure to offer a tempting target for him. His head snapped forward, his tongue lashing at the spot he had chosen. I felt the sharp pain of him teasing me with his teeth. I milked his knot until I was sure he was about to completely lose control. My hand came up to catch the back of his head.

I leaned over to whisper in his ear, "Mark me now or I'll make you cum ten more times."

His teeth against my neck was enough for me to fall right over the edge. I could feel the bond growing moments later, my cock exploding between us. He throbbed inside me as the bond started to settle. His tongue tended to the bite, the feeling making me cum again. I was drifting off to sleep as he lathered his mark.

Chapter 32

Penelope

Checking my phone for the hundredth time, I sighed when there was no message from Dante or his pack. He should have reached out when I didn't come home after work. Typing out a message, I deleted it before typing it out again. My hand hovered over *Send* before Rhys took it out of my hand. "Give it back."

"We are headed to commit a murder; I don't think having a tracking device on is the best idea." I could hear the chimes as he turned it off.

"Where are we going?"

He tossed my phone into the back seat before replying, "I have a lead on the former beta in the first pack that had you."

"You were pretty confident we were going to kill someone."

"I'm confident that my informant told me the truth."

"How confident?" I looked over at him. "People lie under torture all the time."

"My source is his pack's omega."

"And you expect me to believe you don't torture omegas." It hadn't been a question.

He pulled over into a shopping center parking lot, slamming the car into park, he turned his emotionless gaze on me. "Omegas are the most precious people on this planet. What people like this pack, people like that matchmaker," he spat the word out as if it left a terrible taste in his mouth, "do is abhorrent. It makes me sick to think of any omega in their hands, let alone you, little murderess."

"You raped me." My rage was simmering below the surface, and I was so close to losing it on him. "But that wasn't enough, you did something no one else has ever done, you forced your mark on me. I've never felt so violated in my life."

"I would do it again because you're mine. Always have been, always will be."

I sighed, there was no point in arguing with him. "I loved every second of it. That makes me nearly as sick as you."

His hand came out to catch my chin, he turned my head until I was looking at him. "Penelope, there is nothing wrong with you for enjoying what I did to you. It's not an uncommon reaction to what happened."

"I know that. What makes me sick is I want you to do it again."

"That doesn't make you sick." He leaned over and pressed a kiss against my forehead. "It makes you kinky."

"Even if I want it to happen after I kill someone."

"You're perfect." That was enough for him to take the car out of park and pull back onto the street.

He drove us for what seemed like forever, passing through Raleigh and into the Chapel Hill area of the Triangle. Following winding back streets, he pulled up in front of a rustic cabin, surrounded by woods. He cut the lights and parked on the edge of the property. He slid out of the car and toward the trunk. Using the keys, he opened it and started to pull things out. When I finally got the nerve to join him, I saw what he was grabbing. Two cans of gasoline, matches, and cigarettes.

"Are we going to burn him alive?" I asked.

"That's for after, with as much as you squirt when you cum, I can't risk leaving any evidence behind."

I leaned over his shoulder, seeing an array of weapons laid out there. My hands shook as I reached for one of the hatchets inside. Grabbing it by the handle, I was pleased at the heft in my hand. "You never told me what you learned from the matchmaker."

"Far more than you even know. I had thought to keep it from you."

"That won't work out well for you." My arms crossed under my breasts.

"But I decided against it. I figured, instead, I'd fill you in as we kill each of them."

"If I asked you to tell me everything right now, would you?"

He nodded. "I would, but that would mean tonight's kill would have to wait."

"Is it really that bad?" I huffed.

"How much do you remember?"

There wasn't much that was clear after I met the matchmaker. That first pack drugged me and the rest of them kept it up. Mostly, I remembered the pain and the rapes. "Not much."

"If you want to know I'll tell you." He caught my eyes for a moment and I saw love there, and that was terrifying. "But I assure you, I only want to make you a better woman."

"How sure are you that your way is the right one?"

"I'm certain." There was a sureness in his voice that made me want to place my trust in him.

When I finally agreed, we grabbed our weapons and headed toward the secluded cabin. There were no lights as far as the eye could see, leaving us approaching the house in the dim moonlight. The small porch light was doing nothing to fight back the encroaching darkness as Rhys moved to the front door. He had a set of picks in his hand that he used to open the lock with ease. Setting down the arson supplies, we slid into the house, keeping to the shadows as we moved into its depths. He reached back, catching my hand in his and pulling me tightly against his back. I placed a hand on his shoulder, which seemed to satisfy him enough to keep going.

I could hear the shower running as we approached the bedroom. Rhys didn't hesitate as he stretched the rope between his hands and kicked the door open. There was an open shower in the corner that was occupied by a medium sized man. Rhys was on him before he had time to register anything but shock. The alpha wrapped the rope around the other man's neck, pulling him back into the bedroom. They fought for a moment before Rhys cocked his fist back and slammed it into the man's face. He collapsed onto the floor with a satisfying thud.

"I've got this." He knelt, lifting the man before he tilted his head, indicating a bag in the corner. "Check the bag, there should be more rope in there."

Heading to the bag, I opened it, finding a kit complete with rope, duct tape, and blades of all kinds. Reaching in, I selected the duct tape and handed it off to Rhys. He grinned, taking it from me and taping him to the bed with wide bands of it. "Should we wake him up?"

"I was hoping seeing his face would jog your memory."

I studied him for a moment, he was familiar, but I couldn't place it. "I got nothing."

"Not surprised." He moved to the side of the bed and retrieved a syringe set and a vial of something. "Propofol."

"What is that?"

"It's an anesthetic." He pulled a second unmarked vial filled with similarly milky white liquid from inside. "I wager this is methamphetamine."

"How do you know what those are?"

"Their omega told me where to find everything." The man on the bed started to struggle. "I see our captive is awake. Let's see how much we can get him to admit to."

He led me to the bed, keeping me at his side as we reached the beta lying there. His eyes widened as he gasped, "Penelope, you should be dead. They promised to kill you."

"We're going to play a game of truth or bleed," Rhys spoke, taking the attention off of me. "I ask you questions and you tell me the truth or she makes you bleed."

"Fuck you, she's just a whore we purchased."

Rhys slapped him so hard his head bounced against the mattress beneath him. "Don't ever fucking speak about my omega that way."

"You marked a slut who will take any knot she can get."

I had heard enough. Crossing to him, I took the hatchet in my hand, slamming it down on the bed between his legs. I mostly missed his balls, just grazing them enough to make him bleed. "You don't get to speak about me that way. I was only like that because you made me that way."

"Let's start this game." Rhys indicated the opposite side of the bed and I smirked as I took in the space. He handed me a pocket knife across the restrained man. "Now, time for my first question. Tell me the names of your pack members."

"Why should I? You're just going to kill me no matter what I say."

"You're right about that. But telling me the truth just grants you an easy death." My alpha caught my eyes. "Now, when you're cutting along someone's arm, intention matters. If you wish to kill you cut vertically, up the arm and toward the heart. To extract information, it's best to leave a shallow wound, horizontal along the arm."

I nodded, lining the blade up with his arm around the elbow. Pressing the blade into his skin, I got a wicked thrill seeing the blood welling. Pulling the blade along the crook, I watched, mesmerized, as a solid line of deep crimson flooded out when I lifted it. "You fucking bitch!"

I lashed out again, creating another cut just below the first. "Once again, you aren't allowed to speak to me at all, certainly not like that."

"Now, I know who your pack is." Rhys leaned over the beta before continuing. "So, I suppose we will pass on that question, Orion." It sparked joy in my heart to watch the fear in the beta's eyes. "But because you lied to me, you get to help me teach my little murderess something."

Rhys tugged on the beta's shirt, exposing just a little skin. I laughed at his attempts before sliding the blade beneath the cloth and slicing up the center. Orion's chest was exposed, letting me see the quivering of his stomach. "What now?"

"Place the blade against his stomach." I did as he instructed. "Now, on the stomach you can cut deeper than you can on the arms." I pressed the edge in until I watched it disappear. "That's good, hold it right there, any deeper and you perforate the stomach, you don't want to do that. It releases this awful smell."

"Please, I'll tell you anything!" The beta's screams made me wet.

"You have four alphas and an omega." Rhys's voice filled the space as I dragged the blade across his stomach. "Now, I don't punish omegas, so you only have to deal with four cuts. This is the first." Rhys caught my eyes. "The first alpha, Misha, he's the pharmacist. He cooks the meth and steals the propofol."

The line of blood was starting to fall over the beta's sides and collect in a pool beneath him on the mattress. I pulled the blade back enough to see the blood sparkle in the lamp light. "Who else?"

"His second alpha, Adam," I was surer this time. "His job is taming; he likes to break omegas." Rhys was so calm it pissed me off, the blade slipped just a bit deeper by the time I started the third. "Next is Franco, he takes care of the omegas. You don't want him taking care of you." It took everything I had to not sink the blade handle-deep into the beta. "The final one is Vic, he's the ringleader." He caught my eyes as I raised the blade from the last cut. I hesitated to do what I wanted to, my tongue slipping out to wet my lips. "Go ahead."

Rhys's permission was all it took for me to lick along the blade. The coppery taste pulled a long moan from my lips. My eyes closed as I lapped at the blade, collecting as much of it on my tongue as I could. "Fuck, that's good."

"You smell good." The beta's voice made me jump.

The resulting growl from Rhys made my eyes snap open in time for me to watch him snatch the hatchet from the ground and sink it into the beta's skull.

Rhys turned his attention to me then. "You have ten seconds before I start to chase you." That was all it took for me to start running.

Chapter 33

Rhys

Watching my omega disappear around the corner was the most enchanting thing I had seen in a while. I couldn't wait to hunt her down and make her mine all over again. Giving one last look to the beta on the bed, I sighed. I hated to end our game so quickly but there was no way I was letting that scum continue to smell her perfume. Watching her lick the blood off that blade made my cock throb in my pants. I was so close to my rut every time she perfumed. Her heat was coming soon; I could tell that much from the way her scent got sweeter, making me more tightly wound by the moment.

I heard the creak of a door opening, filling me with amusement. My little murderess thought she was slick. My head turned, moving toward the front of the house. The front door was cracked, letting in a beam of light. I studied that door for a moment, trying to puzzle out the trap she had set, for I was sure she hoped to catch me with this. Turning, I started to head up the stairs, hesitating on the third step. I spun in place, heading out that door and slamming it behind me. A muffled curse from my right drew my eyes in that direction, letting me catch a shadow disappearing around the corner of the cabin.

Leisurely strolling after her, I contemplated all the things I would do to her when this finally ended. Turning the corner, I studied that side of the house, there was nothing there but a small strip of grass and a hedge fence. There was enough space at the bottom of the hedge for someone to hide. Leaning down, I scanned along until I felt a smack on my ass and heard a peel of feminine laughter as she ran past me leaving a cloud of perfume in her wake. I popped back up, watching her disappear once again. Shaking my head, I decided I was going to cut her off from the other side. Coming around the front of the house, I passed the open door and went around until I was able to peek around the corner. She was leaning around the back corner of the house, her head disappearing as she peeked. The way she was standing made her ass look rather scrumptious.

Coming up behind her, I leaned down and whispered, "You ready to call game over?"

She released the cutest yelp and took off running in the other direction. I followed her around, close enough behind her that every time she looked over her shoulder she saw me right there. I watched her take the corner to the front of the house, her feet going out from under her before she righted herself and sprinted for the front door. I let her get inside and slam the door behind her. Coming up to it, I grinned as I pulled that door open. My head tilted up so I could watch her disappear up the stairs. I took the steps two at a time, coming to the top and heading toward the only open door. Coming into the room, I pulled the closet door open, smiling when I didn't find her there.

Movement behind me made me spin in place as I watched raven curls disappear into a bedroom. I was right on her heels with a growl of, "You love your alpha chasing you, don't you, little murderess?"

I reached out and grabbed her arm, bringing her close to me. My hands slid down her chest, pulling her shirt off and tossing it into the darkness of the room. Spinning her in my arms, I grabbed ahold of her waist and tossed her onto the bed. I opened my blade with a flick of my wrist and cut her pants off in a few sure strokes. Grabbing her by the thighs, I tugged her down until her knees rested on my shoulders. Kneeling, I pulled her up until she was able to hook her knees over my shoulders. Lifting her into the air, I got a thrill at her scream of fear as she settled there.

I could feel the moment she decided to throw herself backwards, making a split-second decision, I threw my hands up to catch her ass. Pushing her forward, I moaned when I tasted the sweetness of her slick. Sucking her lips into my mouth, I nibbled along them as she shivered above me. She fisted my hair in her hands pushing me harder against her until she was making desperate sounds for me. My tongue darted out, catching her clit. Her whole body shook as I ran my teeth over her clit, I knew that pain turned her on, and I planned on giving her as much of it as she could take.

My hands slid up her body, catching her nipples in my fingers and twisting them. The moan she released was matched by more of that delicious slick. She was perfection as I pushed her over the edge, teasing her clit with quick strokes of my tongue. Her weight fell backwards, and I had to think fast to catch her. Lowering her down onto the bed, I continued to lap at her. Her moans built as I pushed her through three more orgasms, the bed beneath us was soaked.

Her hands moved so she was pushing me away. "No more, please."

"You said you wanted to be taken, I'm taking you." I didn't give her a chance to answer, diving back down to tease her clit again.

Her legs tightened around my head, making me growl against her clit. That was enough to have her tighten her legs around my head. It felt like I was stuck in a vise grip, and I loved every second of it. "Alpha, alpha, alpha."

She repeated it over and over like a prayer as she squirted all over my face. When she released my head, she started to scoot backwards up the bed. "Don't run, little murderess, I'll always catch you."

"Alpha, please."

"Your heat's coming, you're going to need all the orgasms you can get."

"You're going to send me directly into it." She looked desperate.

"Do you want me to stop?"

She thought about that for a moment. "Would you?"

"Not a chance in hell," I growled as I lapped at her clit.

She jumped like I had just struck her. That gave me an idea. Pulling back, I brought my hand down on her clit. Her moan was enough for me to keep going. Using my other hand, I slid two fingers inside her. Her voice was everything as she begged me for mercy, there wasn't anything she could do to get that from me. Twisting my wrist, I followed her as she scooted back until she hit the wall. "Please, alpha."

There was something in her voice that froze me where I was. "Tell me what you need."

"My heat's coming."

"We know that," I growled.

"No, now."

"Then we need to go."

She chewed her lip as I pulled my finger from her. "I need you to order me to wait until we get home."

The enormity of what she was asking slammed into me like a freight train. I didn't even know if she remembered the alphas using their barks to force her to do anything they wanted. It was a common tactic. That was yet another thing I hoped she didn't remember. "Are you sure?"

"I'm not wild about the idea but it's only you and me out here and home is over an hour away."

"I can make it work, call Richie to help you until we can leave."

She took a deep breath before she nodded. "Order me to wait, be specific."

My heart ached that she was asking me to do this. There was only one way for this to work, she had to be unconscious. My voice broke as I mustered every bit of alpha command I could into my bark. "Sleep, little murderess, and wake only in Dante's arms."

Chapter 34

Xavier

Dante was teetering on the edge of his heat. He had begun reorganizing his nest this morning. At the moment, he was teasing Evan's cock with his tongue while the beta begged. Most omegas were docile when they were in heat, Dante was the opposite. He became more aggressive and dominant, demanding what he wanted. We loved every second of it, but I was more concerned now than ever. Penelope was supposed to go into heat any time now if she was to be believed. It wouldn't surprise me if they went at the same time.

Dante reached out to Richie as he crossed the room, but the alpha skirted his touch making the omega whine. Evan redirected him with a hand on his cheek. The other alpha moved beside me, saying, "We have a problem."

"What is it?"

"Rhys called, he's out with Penelope and she started to go into heat." I growled at the thought of her being at the serial killer's mercy. "He ordered her to sleep but I doubt it will last long. He's coming in hot."

"We need to get Dante up to the nest. It's time I deal with Rhys." As if on cue, the front door opened and we were greeted with Penelope in the older alpha's arms. Rage ripped through me when I saw she was unconscious. "What did you do to her?"

He shrugged. "I didn't do anything to her that she didn't ask for."

"As if you asked last time." Richie's snarl nearly made me laugh. There was nothing dominant about that man.

"That doesn't matter here." Rhys looked at me with just an ounce of pleading in his eyes. "We need to get her to the nest."

"Explain it to me like I'm five." I crossed my arms across my chest, catching his eyes and refusing to drop them.

He held my stare for a long moment before looking down at Penelope. "She said she was going into heat. That she wouldn't make it home."

"So why is she unconscious?"

"She asked me to order her to wait until she was home."

"Home." Richie seemed struck by that before a grin spread across his face. "She called us home."

"So, you ordered her to sleep," I snapped at Rhys.

"It was the only way to get her here safely, considering I can't very well see to an omega in heat and drive at the same time."

Richie was staring at her like he was sure something was wrong. "She shouldn't still be asleep."

"My exact order was for her to sleep until she was in Dante's arms." He stared us down. "I think that would be more comfortable for all involved in the nest."

"Fine, but if she doesn't wake up, I'll cut your throat."

"If she doesn't wake up, I'll hand you the knife and bear my throat." He turned and climbed the stairs to the nest.

I went to Dante and Evan, leaning down to whisper in the omega's ear, "Penelope's here."

"Where?"

I smiled, offering him a hand up. "She's in the nest."

He took the hand I offered him and as soon as he was on his feet, he took off running. I was close on his heels, watching as he launched himself onto the bed. I had a moment to take in what Dante had done to the nest. There was a large bank of windows that overlooked Lake Jordan where he had set up a pallet of blankets and pillows. A large bookshelf bed was built into the wall, each shelf occupied by comics and superhero memorabilia. The other wall held an assortment of sex toys.

"What's wrong with Penelope?" Dante was already moving, pulling the other omega into his arms.

The moment he did, she came alive. "I need."

"Tell me what you need, princess." I could tell this was going to be a very different heat than we were used to. Dante was so focused on the other omega and her pleasure that he tuned the rest of us out.

"A knot." It was as close to a whine as I ever wished to hear from her.

Richie and Rhys moved as one. Dante stopped them with a hand in the air. "Richie, help my princess. Me and Rhys need to talk." Richie slid onto the bed, picking her up and carrying her to the nest Dante had created. I looked around, waiting for my omega to speak. Bradley and Evan held just as much suspicion in their gazes as I felt. Who knew what Rhys was thinking. Dante crawled along the bed until he was sitting with his legs hanging over the edge. "We need to make some things clear before this kicks off."

"How has your heat not hit yet?" Rhys's head cocked as if he was studying Dante.

"It's coming, don't you doubt that, and soon. But before I give myself over, I need to set the ground rules."

Rhys huffed, "Who needs rules to fuck?"

"I do," Dante admitted. "They're very simple. You do what the fuck I say. There are no safe words and no ways out. You obey. It's really that simple."

"What if I don't want to?"

"I don't have time for brat taming during a heat," he sighed. "I can already tell this heat is going to be different than any other I've had. All I want is Penelope safe and taken care of."

"Then we have the same goals."

"I won't take kindly to you doing anything she doesn't like."

"Understood." Rhys nodded.

The conversation was cut off by a scream of Richie's name from behind us followed by the room flooding with her scent. That was all it took for Dante to lose himself to his heat. His hands started moving, tearing at his clothes until he stood naked in front of us. The sight sent my cock achingly hard, making me reach for him. "Please, alpha."

I stripped as I moved, lifting Dante and setting him gently on the bed next to Penelope. Her voice was full of sleep when she spoke. "Dante. Good, my alpha did as I asked."

"He did, princess."

"Don't be too hard on him, I asked him to."

He nodded. "Get some sleep, I'll be here when you wake up."

I leaned forward and kissed along his jaw, teasing his throat right above where I marked him all those years ago. He moaned for me, making me nibble at that mark. I loved the sounds he made as he ground himself against me. It was so easy for me to get him all worked up, and I needed him at his most dominant. I needed to prove a point to Rhys. His hands tangled in my hair as I bit down on that mark, making Dante buck against me. His slick covered my stomach like a badge of honor.

He finally broke, hissing out, "Be a good boy and suck my cock."

I laughed as I kissed my way down his chest. Flicking my tongue out, I caught the head of his cock there. His delicious taste exploded on my tongue, making me take him balls deep down my throat. I loved every second of the sounds he made for me. A growl of satisfaction came from me when he murmured, "Good boy."

My tongue swirled around the head of him, making him fall back against the pillow. Motion beside me made me pull back enough to see Bradley coming to take my place, putting his hand on my shoulder and whispering, "You need to keep an eye on Rhys. I've got this."

I pulled off Dante and allowed Bradley to take my place. I pulled Rhys to a corner, "I don't want you here."

"You haven't really hidden that." We both had our eyes glued to the bed, neither of us wanted to let the omegas out of our sight.

"You aren't going anywhere, and neither am I. I suppose it's time we start working together."

He turned his head to actually look at me for the first time. "It hasn't been that long. How do you know I'm not going anywhere?"

"You had your chance to take Penelope and run. You came back here and provided her with what she needed." I finally turned to catch his eyes. "Most alphas wouldn't have brought her back here knowing there was another omega in the house."

"She would have murdered me if I hadn't."

That made me laugh. "I highly doubt that."

"I swear to god, if you don't knot me right this second, Bradley Sean O'Connell, I will tie you up and milk that knot until you pass out!" Dante's threat was met with Bradley flipping him over and slamming his knot home, stretching Dante around him. "Such a good boy."

The alpha rolled Dante to the side where he could reach out and pull Penelope into his arms. "I've certainly never seen anything like that." Rhys commented.

"Not many people have." I made a snap decision. "Come with me. I need to show you something."

Chapter 35

Rhys

Evan closed the door behind us, slipping past Xavier. "I'm going to make food and do last minute prep for us. Don't kill each other."

"This way." Xavier guided me to the opposite end of the house, pushing open a door to reveal a grand library. "We can talk in here."

I didn't see why we needed to leave the nest, but I took a seat by the large window-lined reading nook. Reaching into my pocket, I pulled out my cigarette case and tapped a joint out from inside. "Mind if I smoke?"

"You literally escaped prison..." He held up a hand. "You know what? I don't want to know. It's fine."

"Thanks."

Sparking the end, I watched as he crossed the room and took a seat directly across from me. "There's no easy way to bring this up."

"Which this? The thing where everyone in the house apparently grew up together? Or the thing where I murdered Penelope's mother? Or maybe the one where I raped and marked her by force? Perhaps how your precious Richie and, apparently, your omega lied to you about the alpha's relationship to me?"

"This is a complete fucking mess of a pack." He looked exhausted.

"I've seen worse."

He shook his head. "Whatever happened between you and Penelope is no business of mine, unless it becomes a problem for Dante."

"You don't like Penelope?"

"She's wonderful, don't get me wrong." He seemed to be looking for the right words. "She's just not my type."

"What about a beautiful omega isn't your type?"

"Her gender." He put his hand out for me to pass him the joint. I did so and he hit it a few times before continuing. "I knew Dante was mine from the moment I saw him. There was nothing anyone could do to keep me away from him. Granted, at that point we were literal children, he was all of ten, but there was almost a gravitational pull between us. Dante was always our center."

"Go on." I leaned forward on the table, fascinated by what he was saying.

"There wasn't a time where we didn't have Dante and his twin, Calliope, around us. Penelope came much later. I don't know how much you remember from school, but when puberty hits there starts to be obvious differences between the designations." He took a long pull from the joint before ashing it, reaching over, and gesturing for a new one. "It became abundantly clear that Dante, his twin, and Penelope were omegas, small ones at that."

"That must have caused problems."

"Not as many as you might think. We were all pretty comfortable with each other at that point."

"What happened?"

"I don't completely believe the story Penelope gave us," he sighed. "She and Dante have always shared a special kind of connection. It isn't like anything I've ever seen before. Everything started to change when they got designation tested. Dante's twin was first, and to no one's surprise, she came back an omega."

"Let me guess, Dante wasn't thrilled about that, was he?"

"We were all pretty certain Penelope and Dante were omegas, our omegas, but Dante held onto the hope he would be a beta."

I nearly laughed. "Twins *never* have different designations."

"Love isn't rational." He had a point there. "When his test came back that he was an omega, he wouldn't leave his bed for weeks. Tried to get suppressants, did everything he could to not be who he was. It was heartbreaking to watch."

"What changed?"

"Penelope came back as an omega as well and she had a similar reaction. That seemed to break Dante out of it." He stood and grabbed a book from the shelf before returning to the table and asking, "Have you ever heard the Greek creation myth for our species?"

The change of subject came out of nowhere. "Not much, honestly."

"It was said that when Apollo sculpted humans, we had two heads and four arms and legs. Zeus saw this and struck us apart."

"Then why do so many omegas need a whole pack around them?"

"I'm getting there, be patient," he admonished. "Then, there is the myth of Lycus. He was said to be descended from wolves, of all things. According to myth, it was Lycus that created the first omegas."

"We know that designations aren't ancient, they're relatively new, so that can't be true."

"Why not?"

"Scientific record refutes it." I couldn't believe that I was arguing science versus mythology with him.

"Does it? Or did we just not have sufficiently advanced tests to determine the difference?" He opened the book to a page, spinning it around and offering it to me. "Read this."

I took the book from him, noting the title at the top, DSM-5. I scanned the page, noting some of the main symptoms: *an abnormally high sex drive, repeated sexual experiences that cause distress, seeking sex to the point that it's a detriment to their wellbeing*. My eyes moved to the top of the page, reading the diagnosis as Hypersexual Disorder. My eyes traveled up until I was looking at Xavier. "That sure as fuck sounds like an omega in heat without a pack."

"My thoughts exactly." He took the book back and flipped to another page. "Now read this."

A person with Dependent Personality Disorder has an obsessive need to be taken care of, they may be described as clingy or needy by those around them. An intense fear of abandonment. "I don't know if I would say Penelope was like this." He crossed his arms over his chest and stared down at me. "But that does kind of sound like an omega."

"Exactly." He took the book and placed it back on the shelf.

"What was that?"

"An antique diagnostic manual for mental illnesses." He took a seat across from me again. "Some of them, we still use, others were just from lack of a better term."

"Is there anything in there that sounds like alphas?"

"Not that I've found." His hand came to his temple and he started to rub in small circles. "That's the thing about mental health; the diagnoses change all the time as society and science evolves."

"What does any of this have to do with the omegas?"

"*Our* omegas." he stared at me pointedly, "provide a unique opportunity for us."

"What's that?"

"Omega pairings are pretty rare, but most of them don't have children with each other. According to myth and papers I found a few years ago, when two omegas have children, they always have triplets, one of each designation."

"You want to experiment on our omegas?"

"God no." His denial was too quick for my liking. "But if it comes up it would be interesting to see the results."

"You're just as fucked up as I am."

His laugh filled the room. "They've known about this since high school."

Chapter 36

Dante

Watching Penelope ride Rhys was making my cock achingly hard. My head turned as I watched Xavier come at me. "Kneel."

He fell to his knees, looking up at me with adoration in his eyes. Sitting back on his ankles, he watched as I moved from the bed, but Penelope's whine of, "Don't go," kept me where I was.

"I need you, alpha."

"I'm here, my love." His words were filled with promise.

I held my hand out to him and he came to me, climbing onto the bed between my legs, he started to tease my cock with his tongue. The warmth as he wrapped his lips around me made my toes curl. He knew exactly what I needed, and he gave it to me. Reaching up to wrap his hand around my balls, he tugged just enough for me to start fucking his face. He moaned around me, the sound vibrating down my shaft. My breath sped up to match Penelope's beside me, she was so close to cumming, all I needed to do was push her over that edge. She needed it more than I did.

I let that thought pass, and I reached over and slapped her clit. She moaned for me, her hips moving as she tried to work Rhys' knot into her. My hand slid down until I could work two fingers into her, beside where the alpha's knot was stretching her. My thumb teased her clit as I felt her tighten down around my fingers, her s lick gushing out of her as she pushed them out. Rhys slid the rest of the way inside her, letting her collapse from the overwhelming pleasure of it.

"I can't keep doing this." Her words came out breathy. "My heats are getting out of control. One of you should get me pregnant."

I struggled to breathe as my cock exploded down Xavier's throat at the thought. "Fuck, princess, you can't be talking that way."

"But I wanna make you daddy, Dante."

Rhys' laugh made me give him a dirty look. "We can discuss this after your heat."

"But, Dante." That whiny pout made me laugh.

"It's final."

"Fine. We can discuss it in the morning." She turned her head and fell asleep on Rhys' chest.

"Fucking finally," I sighed.

"You aren't in heat anymore?" Xavier's voice made me look at him.

"Mine ended two days ago. You can't tell?"

Bradley answered as he came into the room with food, "You've been different this heat. Less intense, almost normal."

"It's Penelope," I admitted. "Something about her being here with us finally. I just feel settled."

Bradley set the tray by the bed and offered me his hand. I took it and allowed him to lift me off my feet and carry me into the living room where Richie and Evan were sitting. Xavier took a seat and pulled me into his lap as soon as he was comfortable. "We need to talk about what Penelope just said."

"I don't know that we do." I cut Xavier off before he could continue. "There seems to be a fundamental misunderstanding about the hierarchy in this house, and I am correcting it right now."

"I just meant—"

"You just nothing. This isn't something we discuss without her present, if and only if she brings it up. Have I made myself clear?" When they didn't respond, I continued. "You all think she is the pack's second omega, that's where you're wrong. She is my mate."

"The fuck she is," Rhys snapped as he came into the room.

"She might be yours..." I nodded at the alpha. "But you aren't her mate. I am. And I don't give two fucks if I have to kill each and every one of you, she will not be hurt."

"We don't intend to harm her, love." Xavier's voice made my head turn.

"Stop playing the peacemaker."

He lifted me, setting me down so I was looking at him. "What's wrong?"

"I don't know and it's pissing me off."

"You should be ecstatic," Richie commented. "Penelope literally said she wanted to make you a father."

"That was just her heat talking."

"What if it wasn't?" Xavier was the last person I expected to be pressing this.

Rhys chose that moment to cut in. "I know this is only her first or second heat with this pack, but she has had her heats abused to no end."

"Go on." He had all of my attention.

"When these people take omegas, one of the most common tactics is having alphas use their barks to force an omega into heat. Once a heat starts, they aren't let free of it until they are sold. It takes a toll on a person, whether they remember it or not. Pregnancy is one of the few ways to get a break from that."

"How about we split the difference," I suggested. "You guys get the shot now and keep it going, and we just wait and see if she brings it up."

"Brings what up?" Penelope murmured as she came out of the nest. Her hair was wet, as if she had just showered. There was no way she had gotten enough sleep.

I slipped out of Xavier's lap and went to her. "What are you doing up, princess?"

"The bed was cold. Brings what up?"

"Let's go back to bed." I tossed a scowl over my shoulder at my pack. "I'll get Richie to bring us some food."

"What were you guys talking about?"

"Let's get comfortable."

She let me lead her to the bed, I couldn't help shaking my head and stripping the bed. The pillows and blankets ended up in a pile by the door. It was the slick-soaked sheets that needed to be stripped. I didn't have the patience for this. A growl ripped from my lips as I grabbed her hand and pulled her from the room. We almost ran directly into Richie and his plate of food. "What's wrong?"

"It's filthy, headed to the basement." I pushed past the men in the living room and pulled open the basement doors. Penelope laughed as I pulled her down those stairs and into the basement nest. The bed was in the corner next to a large window that opened to the backyard. I loved this part of the house, I had chosen it because it was built into a hill. Moving to the bed, I smiled when I saw my pack coming with armfuls of blankets and pillows. Releasing Penelope's hand, I went to Xavier, taking a pile of blankets from his arms and pressing a kiss to his cheek. "Thank you."

Dropping the blankets at the end of the bed, I crawled along its length until I was comfortable leaning against a stack of pillows. "You've tried to distract me long enough, what are we not talking about until I bring it up?" Penelope crossed her arms across her chest.

"What do you remember about being with Rhys earlier?"

She smirked as she crawled onto the bed. Watching her come toward me with so much confidence and love in her eyes made me rock hard. She stopped when she was on all fours above me, her face pressed against mine when she whispered, "I would very much like if you got me pregnant, my love."

"I won't go back into heat for at least three months."

She rolled to my side, allowing me to pull her into my arms. "That gives me a bit of time to finish what I started, before I have to take a break."

I wasn't sure what she meant by that, but it sure would be fun to find out.

Chapter 37

Penelope

Rhys' hand in mine as we watched the alpha clean out his car was centering to me. I didn't know what it was about this alpha that made me weak, but it wasn't something I wanted to explore right now. I was entirely too vulnerable to allow myself to be distracted by him no matter how much I might like to. There was entirely too much at stake for me to let my hormones run rampant. Rhys had his arm around me, making me feel way more comfortable than I should have been. I couldn't imagine my life without him now. The thought made my heart ache.

He had made it clear I was his, but could he really be mine?

Not in the same way Dante was, but mine in his own way. He did fill a void I didn't even know I had in my life. His warmth was something I had long grown used to, falling asleep on his bulk was easy, he was as soft as he looked. I had come to find that his was the first face I looked for in the morning after Dante's. I was falling for this dangerous man, and I was falling hard.

"He's on the move." Rhys' whisper made me focus on the man we were stalking. He led me to the car, silently pulling in behind the alpha. We drove for a while before he started to speak. "This man is the accountant."

"I find it hard to believe that an organization that sells humans has an accountant."

"I use that in the loosest terms." He laughed. "He's the money man. If it costs anything, he handles it." He reached over and grabbed my hand. "I think this is the one we bring the pack in on."

That made me snap my head toward him. "They know I'm killing people."

"There's knowing and then there's seeing."

"I don't want to lose Dante when I've just found him again."

He brought my hand up to his lips, pressing a gentle kiss to my fingers. "You want to say yes."

"Yes." That was all it took for my nerves to act up.

Dante

Xavier held me in his arms as we sat in the back of Richie's SUV waiting for Penelope to call us. I loved being surrounded by my men; this was the first time in a long time that I had really felt at peace. For a long time, I had blamed that on the men, and then my own failings. Now, I realized we were missing a piece of our puzzle. A Penelope shaped piece, to be exact. Things were just more comfortable with her around. Her relationships with some of them were a little strained, but they would work that out in time.

Moments passed, cocooned in Xavier's scent as I was before my phone started to ring, all the apprehension I had been feeling evaporated as soon as I heard Penelope's voice. "We're ready for you." She hung up before I could reply.

Richie cranked the car and pulled out into the road. We drove in circles as we followed the directions Rhys was texting me. We ended up in front of what appeared to be a decaying farmhouse on a patch of land that backed up to a large, wooded thicket on all sides. It was like they had carved the plot of land out specifically for this house. It was the perfect place to commit a murder, if one was so inclined. My eyes scanned the area until I spotted the barn. If the house looked like it was decaying, the barn looked like it was about to collapse. Rhys was coming from that barn with his arm around Penelope's shoulders. They seemed more comfortable with each other than ever before. She was leaning into him, her arms wrapped around his waist. I would have to get her alone soon and make sure she was okay.

She pulled away from the alpha, coming to me and wrapping herself around me. Their scents had mixed together in a not unpleasant way. "I'm so glad you're here." Her voice galvanized me, making me tighten my arms around her.

"Show me what you have."

"Are you sure?" She pulled back enough to catch my eyes. "You can leave now without getting involved, it won't hurt my feelings."

"Princess, I love you. Not just on your good days but also on your bad. I love all the parts of you, including the darkness." My eyes came up so I could look at Rhys as I spoke the next words. "Rhys provides something for you that I can't, that no one else in the pack can. If that's something you both wish to share with us, who are we to object?"

"Do you all feel that way?" Rhys spoke for the first time.

Xavier stepped up, his voice deep and calm as he responded. "We do. This wouldn't be the first murder we were at least a little complicit in."

Rhys nodded before turning and going back into the barn. Penelope stepped from my grasp and took my hand as we followed the alpha, our pack standing at our backs. I felt invincible, and that was a rare thing. She hesitated at the doors, her hand stalled on the wood. She took a deep breath before she pushed it open. I was carefully blank as I took in the scene before me. They had an alpha hung in a giant X formation, his chest a pattern of wounds. I traced the wound path in my mind, trying to work out what weapon had caused them. Something with a jagged edge. A hunting knife perhaps.

"What did he do?" I had to know.

"He's the money man." Rhys responded. "We already got everything off him that we could."

"I'm sure."

"You think you could do better?"

I laughed; it was fun to watch it play across the alpha's face. "There's an art to breaking a person. And while you seem to have the physical part of it in hand, the psychological aspect is much more difficult."

He gestured to the man. "By all means..."

I shrugged, stepping from Xavier's arms, and headed toward the alpha. My hand came back, one of my alphas placed a bottle of water in it. Opening it with a flick of my thumb, I dumped its contents over the alpha's head, making his eyes shoot open. "Oh good, you're awake."

"Just kill me," he begged. No, that just wouldn't do.

"But we were just getting ready to let you go."

"Really?"

Hope sparkled in his eyes. "Of course. There's just one thing I need to do first."

I moved behind him, my hand finding the switch blade at my side. Kneeling down, I opened the blade and placed it along his Achilles tendon. The slice I made on each of them was clean; his scream made my heart sing. Coming back around him, I nodded to Rhys. "Let him go." He did as I asked, and the alpha decided he was going to try and run. All that did was result in him face planting into the concrete. "Now, the rules are simple. If you can walk out of the barn, you're free to go."

"And I thought I was evil." Rhys smirked at me.

Chapter 38

Dante

When Penelope drove her blade through the alpha's head, I couldn't have been more relieved. The way she perfumed while she took his life had me intrigued. "Want to play a game?"

She turned, leaving the axe buried in the alpha's skull. "What kind of game?"

"A hunt." Her eyes widened the moment I said it. "You and me versus the pack."

She hesitated for a moment before a wicked grin crossed her face. "Run."

"You heard her, boys, run." They didn't hesitate, turning as one and disappearing into the property. I started counting in my head, and when I got to ninety, I held my hand out to Penelope. "Let's go get them."

We walked hand in hand out of the barn, I scanned the space as we moved. There weren't too many places they could hide. The most obvious ones would be out of the question. Our men knew I would think to check there first, and they would hide accordingly. Or they wouldn't bother. That much was evident by the blur that ran around the corner. Penelope pulled from me, heading around the other side of the house. I knew what her plan was immediately, I headed around the back, following the path they had taken.

Rounding the corner, I made it in time to catch Evan turning around to head toward me. I reveled in the panic in his eyes when he saw me coming as he turned in place and sprinted toward me. Locking eyes with Penelope, I winked at her as we moved as one, sprinting to meet him in the middle. She launched herself at his back as I wrapped myself around his knees. He fell, but somehow managed to wrap himself around Penelope while he held me to him, protecting us both so he took most of the impact. He seemed to need a moment when we came to rest, holding both of us close to him. When he released us, I caught her eyes and we both burst out laughing.

"That was too easy," she said through her laughs.

"I was expecting more of a chase." I looked down at Evan from where I was standing. "Come on, you get to watch the rest of it."

"Oh no, you discovered my plan," he feigned offense.

I caught something out of the corner of my eye that made my head turn as I tracked movement across the yard. Flaming red hair told me it was Bradley. He was sure to put up more of a chase. I turned to head after him, turning back to see that Penelope was already moving. If I had to wager, she had spotted Richie. I jogged slowly, tracing Bradley's path as I moved. Coming around the front of the house, I saw him sprinting across the open field toward the tree line. I kicked it into gear, eating up the ground between us. He was huffing heavily as he tried to make the tree cover. It was adorable that he thought he could get away from me. The crunching of dry leaves beneath his feet told me he had made it into the woods.

I slowed my pace as I entered the wooded area. I was able to see he was circling the property, trying to place where everyone was. Staying a few steps behind him, my eyes moved to the open space. Evan was standing at Penelope's side as she rested with Richie. Bradley was trying to hide from me, the thought was adorable, there wasn't anything he could do to keep me from him.

I picked my way through the forest until I was staring at his back. Hiding behind one of the trees, I reached down and grabbed a pinecone. My aim was impeccable when I tossed it behind the alpha. His head spun as he bolted, running right toward me. He passed me, turning back. I was able to see the sparkle in his eyes telling me he was enjoying himself as much as I was. I launched myself at him, pouncing on his back and riding him to the ground. He reached back, snatching me off him and rolling to the side so I was beside him.

His laugh was deep, edged with just a little bit of that toe- curling growl. "You got me. Who's left?"

I did a mental tally in my head. "Just Rhys and Xavier."

"Come on." He grabbed my hand, leading me out of the woods.

Penelope jumped when Richie tapped her shoulder, her head turning as she rewarded me with one of her megawatt smiles. She stepped away from the alpha, running to me at full speed. She launched herself into the air, I wasn't sure who she was aiming for, but I stepped in front of Bradley, my arms out. Her weight when she landed made me spin in place, adjusting my stance as I moved. She buried her head against my throat, letting out a sigh of relief when she pressed a kiss there.

"Princess." My words were stolen from me when her perfume bloomed around us.

She cut me off before I could finish my thought. "I'm so horny."

I reacted instantly, carrying her to the back of the house. Evan and Richie had taken places around the firepit there. They watched us come around the house, their eyes tracking every move we made. There was a hunger there that made my heart race. We moved across the clearing, Bradley sliding in behind me so he took the chair. I slid to the ground, keeping Penelope in my lap as I moved. The heat coming from between her legs was making my cock throb. I wanted so desperately to be buried there.

"Talk to me princess." I needed her words now more than ever.

"I want..."

I leaned back so I could catch her eyes. "Tell me what you want."

"A knot."

"Bradley, you're up." I delegated as quickly as I could. When she started whining at that, I turned back to her. "Did you not want Bradley?"

"I want your knot, but his bite."

I smiled at that; omega hormones really were a monster of their own. "I don't have a knot, but..." I held my hand up making sure the whole thing was visible to her. "We could try a substitute."

Her eyes widened, "Yes, that."

My hands moved, pulling her shirt over her head and tossing it aside. Her shorts were next, leaving her exposed pussy in front of my face. I moved without a thought, reaching up and grasping her ass. Burying my face there, I lapped along her lips with my tongue, catching her slick on my tongue as she dripped for me, it was delicious. I held back my moan long enough to wrap my lips around her clit. My tongue caught the tip of her, my moan making my tongue vibrate against her. She pushed against me, making her fall forward into Bradley's lap. I pressed the advantage I had, sliding two fingers inside her and arching them toward me.

Chapter 39

Penelope

Dante was driving me wild with the way he was working me. Every movement of his fingers against my g-spot sent pleasure shooting through me. He twisted his hand, the stretch of his movement making me fall against Bradley's chest. He reached down, catching my chin in his hand, he tilted my head up so I could see his sparkling emerald eyes. "You're safe with us, little one, you can fall apart."

It was like a switch flipped in my head; my orgasm made my legs shake so bad my left one nearly gave out as I gushed for them. Dante caught my leg, setting my foot on his shoulder. He shifted enough to be able to slide a third finger into me. The stretch made me ache for more; I needed more. My head came up as I caught Bradley's eyes, my hands slid up his thighs until I could undo his belt and pull his cock out. Leaning down, I wrapped my lips around him, savoring his taste for a moment before swallowing him to his knot. His hands found the back of my head as Dante worked his fingers inside me. The sensation of being filled made me tighten around those fingers. He twisted his hand, stretching me. The feeling was enough to make me cum again. I came off Bradley's cock with a high, helpless moan.

"You're so beautiful." His words made me look at him. "Look at everyone, so enraptured with you." My head turned to catch the rest of the pack as they watched us, everyone had their cocks in their hands, even Rhys. I wasn't sure when he had joined us, but I was relieved to see him.

I didn't see Xavier, but I knew he was there from the way Dante moaned, "Fuck, that feels so good, alpha."

"They can't keep their eyes off you." Bradley's voice made me turn back to him. It was perfectly timed as Dante worked a fourth finger inside me. This orgasm was more intense than the last ones, making me collapse against the alpha. My head landed next to his. "Isn't this just a perfect position?" He leaned over, catching some of my skin in his lips. His tongue lashed out, making my legs start to shake again as Dante worked me up to another orgasm.

"Please." I didn't know who I was talking to, but I needed more.

Dante took the cue before Bradley did, pushing his thumb into the space between his fingers. The alpha released the skin he had, making me whine for him. "Are you sure you want me to claim you?"

"If you don't, I'm going to be pissed," I snarled at him.

He took the note, his head coming forward to claim that spot again. His teeth raked against me, making me clench around Dante. I was so close; Dante was keeping me right at the edge of cumming. My hand came up to catch the back of Bradley's head as he pulled back with my skin between his teeth. I needed his bite more than anything at that moment. He seemed to sense it, leaning back in and biting down. The feeling was nothing like what I had felt with Rhys, the bond blooming between us making the edging even more infuriating. Dante leaned forward and blew on my clit, that was all it took for me to explode around his hand, allowing him to slide all the way inside me. His knuckles brushed the same places a knot did, making me flood for him. Bradley pulled back enough to lap at his mark. The orgasm intensified until darkness claimed me.

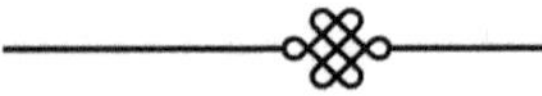

Days later, I was still getting used to the feeling of my bond with Bradley. The one I had with Rhys was so different, quieter. I couldn't tell if he felt nothing, or he was just really good at shielding. I wasn't sure which answer I was more afraid of. Bradley was so vibrant and full of life. His emotions were flooding over, right now, I was a little giddy, but that was just because his contentment was bleeding through. I could feel Dante if I really tried to, and he seemed more at peace than ever before. There was only one more alpha that would want to claim me, and I wasn't sure if Richie could wait. Not that he would try to rush me if I wasn't ready. I craved his bite more than any of the others, but I needed time for the bond with Bradley to set in.

I was nearing my turn into work when my phone rang. "Yeah?"

"Are you close?" My supervisor's voice came over the speaker.

"I'm about to pull in."

"Good, there's someone here for a sit along that I need you to bring up." I could hear the joy in her voice. "She requested you."

She hung up before I could reply, but it didn't matter, I spotted Amani's car as soon as I pulled in. There was no doubt in my mind that Dorian was in there with her. Parking my car, I got out, coming around to stand beside her car. Her alpha got out first and went around to open her door for her. She moved past him, her head held high as she pulled me into a hug. "I hope you don't mind doing this for me."

Dorian came to join us, standing between us and the entrance. "You know I don't like this."

"Dorian, please." Amani pulled from my arms to turn and face him. "We talked about this." He snarled at her and she moved across the space, getting in his face, her own slightly higher pitched growl trickling from her lips. "You seem to have a fundamental misunderstanding of how this works. I do whatever the fuck I want."

She spun back, sliding her arm through mine so we could link elbows as she moved us toward the building. I managed to pull my arm from hers long enough to scan my key card and get into the building. The guard at the desk didn't even look up at us as we moved past him to the elevator. I had never been more relieved for dispatchers to have our own elevator. My eyes scanned the room as we stepped out onto the floor. I swept past the other dispatchers toward my station in the back corner. Reaching for my headset, I hesitated for a moment, coming to my feet and smiling when I saw my supervisor heading toward me with a head set for Amani. She handed it to me and I got it hooked into my system.

I turned to her, a soft smile on my face. "Are you sure about this?"

"I am."

"Okay, but this isn't anything like you might expect."

"I can handle it," she affirmed.

I had to take her at her word. Turning back to my screens, I took a deep breath before logging into the queue. The line picked up immediately. "911, what's your emergency?"

"I need cops and fire, send everybody!" The male voice was panicked.

"I need your address and the nature of your emergency."

He spat the address out, continuing with, "They're fighting again. I'm afraid he's going to kill her."

"Police are on the way."

"Good."

I sensed he was about to hang up, so I pressed on. "I need you to stay on the line until police get there. Tell me what's happening."

He walked me through everything he heard; it was heartbreaking to hear what was happening, knowing on the other side of that line, an omega was likely losing their life. I managed to hang on until he hung up when the cops arrived. "Are they always like that?"

Amani's voice made me jump. "Not always. But you have to understand that we meet people for a split second on what is often the worst day of their lives. As a dispatcher, we have to be mostly impartial. And calm."

"How do you do it?"

"Sometimes it's hard, a lot of us are in therapy. But mostly you try to not hyperfocus on any one call." I reached out and took her hand. "A lot of people leave after the first rough call. There is no shame in that."

"I'm good."

I smiled at her before taking the next call. "911 what's your emergency?"

"Can you help me?" The voice held an accent that I couldn't quite place.

"I can. Tell me what's going on."

"They beat her, it's not good." There was something close to panic in his voice. "I don't know if she's going to survive this one."

"Can you tell me where you are?" He gave me the address. "Okay, can you tell me anything else."

"Don't send the cops."

"Is there something I need to be aware of?" I could tell from the fear in his voice that there was.

"They're the ones that took us."

The sharp inhale from Amani made me look over at her. "Took you? You were kidnapped?"

"Yes, but they sold us." I could hear Amani typing beside me, her fingers moving at a speed I couldn't quite process.

Chapter 40

Dante

Richie came into the room, there was anger in the way he carried himself. "We got work."

"What's going on?" Xavier pulled me to my feet as he rose.

"Amani texted." My alpha's growl started, so Richie quickly finished. "We don't need to rescue her, don't worry."

"What's going on?" I broke into the conversation, I couldn't have them fighting each other.

Richie offered me a smile before he replied, "She called in a rescue for someone that called for help."

"What do you need from me?"

"I don't know yet." His words made me hesitate. "But I'm sure there will be someone that needs your talents."

"Being the only omega on a team of alphas isn't a talent." I rolled my eyes.

Xavier spoke before Richie could reply, "We can get the rest of this ironed out on the way there."

"About that," Richie said, "I don't think it's a good idea if you come with us."

"What are you talking about? I always breach."

Richie shot me a look before he replied. "It might be time for a change."

"That makes no sense," Xavier snapped. "I'm better prepared for it than anyone else."

I placed my hand on Xavier's arm. "I'm sure there's a reason he wants to change things around."

"There is." Richie seemed to collect himself. "I don't think it's a good idea for you to be involved at all."

"If Dante is going, so am I. You might as well tell me what's going on," Xavier snarled.

When Richie didn't answer, I pressed him. "Tell us, 'cause I sure as shit don't like the way you're hedging around it."

"It's the cops." That was enough for me to pay closer attention. "Someone called dispatch for help, Penelope is still on with them. They said not to send the police."

"And that means keeping Xavier out of this how?"

"They said the cops were the ones that took and were selling them."

I nodded, finally understanding what the alpha was trying to accomplish. "Right call, Richie." He rewarded me with a smile as I turned to Xavier. "He's right, you can't breach. Hell, I don't know if I even want you coming with us."

"You don't get to decide what I do."

I turned enough to be able to place my hand on his chest. "Even one second of hesitation from our enemies can give us the edge we need to survive. You know that as well as I do. As much as I wish it wasn't true, you won't have that moment. Alpha, please, I can't lose you."

"I'm going with you," he decreed. "I won't let my omega go unprotected, but I will stay in the van."

Twenty minutes later, with Richie behind the wheel, we were sitting in front of Amani's shelter waiting for Dorian to join us. I was as relaxed as I was going to get in Xavier's arms. He was tense, his arms tightening around me more as time passed. He always got especially cuddly when he was nervous. It was one of his more endearing qualities. The overhead light came on as another omega and two alphas climbed into the back. I wasn't sure what to think about the new arrivals. The omega was small, shying away from my pack and claiming a spot against the back wall. The alpha had an aura of danger about him, his eyes moving along my pack as if he was looking for weakness.

I pulled Xavier's arms tight around me, seeking comfort from the only person I knew would give it to me. Dorian's eyes moved across us, he hesitated when he saw me pushing back against Xavier. "Dante."

"Dorian." I nodded to him. "Who's the other alpha?"

"That's Ares. He's complicated." Dorian's explanation made me take a second look at Ares, there was nothing about him that was outwardly threatening. Nothing that would make me uncomfortable, but he had an aura about him that made all my instincts scream for me to run.

We traveled in silence, my pack staring Ares down. They could all tell how uncomfortable I was, and it was making them more aggressive. Bradley was the most obvious of them, eyeing the other alpha like he was debating the most painful ways to take Ares apart. And Bradley had the knowledge to do it. Xavier seemed to be paying more attention to me than Ares, but I knew how quickly he could move, and my alpha would do anything to protect me, that much I was certain of. Moments passed as Richie circled the block, looking for somewhere he could park and be hidden. He finally settled on a spot around the corner from the address Amani had sent. Leaning forward, I pulled out of Xavier's arms so I could look out of the window.

The area around us was surrounded by warehouses, there wasn't much to see, but I scanned the area, needing to see what was happening around us. Something made me turn in time to see Ares reaching for the door handle. Xavier's hand was on his wrist, pushing him away from me. My alpha's growl was deep and threatening. There was nothing about this he liked in the least.

Richie

I turned back in time to watch Ares reach for the door handle. The door that Dante was currently looking out of, Xavier moved before any of us, catching the alpha's arm and shoving him away from our omega.

"You don't get to be that close to my omega." There was a clear threat in Xavier's words.

Dorian laughed, "I told you they were possessive."

I rolled my eyes, reaching up to turn off the overhead lights before I slipped from the van. By the time I came around the car, Dorian and Ares were standing on the side of it as Bradley crawled out. It took moments for Evan and Rhys to join them. Taking in the group, I started to strategize. Rhys and Ares would make one hell of a team if what I suspected about the new alpha was true; they carried themselves the same way, their eyes filled with nothing but the potential for death. Bradley would need to stay close to me, the caller said they needed medical help, so that was a necessity. Evan would be sent off into the night, his eye through the scope of his rifle would keep us all safe. That meant Dorian was with me.

I gave them their orders, taking my time to explain every part of this for Rhys and Ares. They took off to wreak havoc as far as I could tell. I doubted they were capable of much else. Dante leaned out; his eyes filled with nothing but concern for us. "Come back to me."

Chapter 41

Rhys

I eyed Ares as we moved through the darkness, there was something about the way he carried himself that reminded me of the men I had shared a prison cell with. Full of the knowledge and power that taking many lives gives you. His head turned so he could catch my eyes; we were about the same age, making me wonder if we had shared a hunting ground at some point. That would make sense; there was one kill of mine that the news linked to another killer. Something about a man who tortured betas. That victim had been a beta, so it tracked. Movement ahead of us made both our heads turn as we tracked the person causing the disturbance.

The sounds of boots shuffling against the concrete told me that there were many people moving as quickly as they could, not caring if they gave away their position. Ares and I moved at the same time, coming around the corner to catch the end of the procession. There was a truly astounding number of uniformed police officers closing in on the warehouse. And we couldn't let them get there. I slid in behind the last man, Ares mimicking my move. My blade was in my hand, and I pulled it across my chosen victim's throat with glee. The other alpha snapped his victim's neck, we shared a smile before we dropped the bodies to the ground. We were moving before the rest of them turned, I ducked into the warehouse closest to us, making sure to kick the rusted metal on the floor as I moved.

I had enough time to hide in the shadows by the door before five men came sweeping in. Waiting until the last one was inside, I pushed the door shut, making the darkness close in on us. I was in my element, using the little bit of light coming in from a high window to navigate my way around. I slid in behind the last officer, catching his shoulder in my hand and spinning him around. His head was exposed, making it easy for me to bury the blade in his skull. My foot connected with his chest, sending him falling back as I retrieved my knife. He made an awful racket when he landed, the yells of his teammates allowing me to pinpoint their locations.

I charged the one closest to me, catching the side of his head with a mean roundhouse kick. Following him to the ground, I slammed the blade through the body armor he wore, sinking it up to the handle. Twisting the blade as I retrieved it, I was moving before the shooting started. They were firing blind, aiming toward the sound of their comrade dying. The muzzle flashes gave them away, allowing me to come around the edges of the chamber and get behind them. Working my way through them one at a time I enjoyed every moment of taking their lives. Coming up behind the last officer, he turned at the last moment; the light from above allowed him to see me coming. His gun was up as he aimed down its length at me.

Penelope

My heart skipped a beat as I watched the progress of the units on my screen. I could track what my pack was doing by the way the police called out over the radio. They were trying to flank my pack, and it wasn't working. Two groups had peeled off, heading off toward the empty warehouses. They were picking them off one by one, the moment they called out Rhys' name my heart jumped into my throat. Pain slammed into me before cutting off so abruptly that I struggled to breathe for a moment as the world closed in around me. Amani was talking to me, but it sounded like she was coming from down a long hallway. Panic settled in as I stood, then started moving across the room in long strides.

She was close behind me, making up some explanation to my supervisor as we stepped into the elevator. My supervisor called out, "Take all the time you need, your job will be here when you get back."

I didn't have the energy to reply, my mind was on Rhys and his clear injury. I needed to get to him, and I needed to do it now. My phone started ringing as we got into my car. Amani was driving as we pulled off. Answering the phone, I pressed it to my ear, "Hello?"

"Rhys has been shot." Dante's words made the breath rush from my lungs. "We have him. Bradley's stitching him up."

"I'm on my way."

"You can't!" His panic made me think.

"Why not?"

He seemed much calmer than he should have been. "We need you to go with Amani and get the shelter ready."

I cursed under my breath, my stomach rolling as nausea threatened to overwhelm me. I'd been tired lately, too tired. It hadn't been long since my last heat and it made no sense that I was aching like I was about to go into it again. It had to be from Rhys' wound, I had to be feeling what he was. That was the only explanation that made sense. Amani had driven us to her shelter in the time I was thinking; there was something in her demeanor that was making me nervous. She parked and came around, pulling open the door for me and offering me her arm. I felt like I was walking through a fog as she led me inside. There was always something so calming about her presence, her just being here with me allowed the panic to recede enough to breathe when she led me down to her home beneath the shelter.

I took a seat on the couch as Amani moved into the kitchen. She took some time heating food up. The smell of it was making my stomach roll. I had to fight not to gag as she carried the plate over and set it in front of me. I pushed it away without even picking up the fork. "I'm not hungry."

"Okay, that's it." She marched to the bathroom and came back with a box. Setting it in front of me, her voice when she spoke was so close to a bark it made me jump. "Take this."

My pulse quickened as I stared down at the box. "I can't be pregnant."

"What makes you say that?"

"I was just in heat."

She crossed her arms, staring down at me like she was scolding a child. "All the more reason to take it."

Twenty minutes later I was staring at the plus sign on that small strip of plastic. I should be happy about this, should love this idea. But there was a knot of doubt in my gut. There were only so many of my pack that could be the father. And one of them had just been shot. My eyes moved up until I was looking at Amani where she stood beside me.

"Could it be wrong?" I half hoped it was.

"It's possible," Amani replied. "You'll have to get someone to double check. I'm sure Bradley would be happy to take a look."

Chapter 42

Dante

While Bradley patched Rhys up, the rest of my pack, along with Dorian and Ares, had cleared the area for me to come in. Richie came to the van door himself to walk me in. He was calmer than anyone else would have been as he spoke to me. "They're in the basement. We tried to go down there but they lost it. Their panic is setting all of us off."

"I got this." I assured him as he led me to the basement door.

Going down the stairs, I paused when I had a full view of the space. Metal bars lined one side of the room, each of them stuffed to the brim with bodies. There were so many that I couldn't make out individuals. As I crossed the room to approach the closest cell, pausing there, I took a moment to figure out what I was seeing. This one was just as full as the others, but it was filled with children. My stomach rolled as I crossed through and pulled the door open. I was relieved to find my men had already opened them.

There were too many eyes in small faces looking up at me in fear. The pain in those many eyes made me take a step back. I sat at their level and waited for one of them who was curious enough to approach me. It took what felt like ages before one of them got the courage to walk out of the cage. The boy was so filthy

I couldn't make out anything but scared blue eyes in a face caked with dirt. He crossed the room slowly, coming to rest just feet from me. His eyes fell to the floor as he kicked out, it was a nervous gesture, and it made my heart ache.

"Are you going to hurt us?" Tears sprang into my eyes when he asked that.

I refused to look away from him as the tears started to fall,. "No one is ever going to hurt you again."

"Do you mean that?"

"I do." I wish I could promise him, but that would be irresponsible of me. "As long as I'm alive, no one will ever hurt you again."

He studied me for a moment before he nodded. "Okay."

He seemed so much older than he appeared. He couldn't have been more than twelve. My eyes moved along the children behind him as they pushed through the doors, flooding into the space. "I need you to go upstairs, can you all do that for me?"

"They don't want us to leave the basement without them."

"You don't have to worry about them anymore." I moved slowly as I came to my feet, hoping not to startle the group. Turning around, I headed to the bottom of the stairs and called up. "Richie, can you come down here for a moment?"

He came down the stairs slowly, his eyes moving along the children behind me. "Jesus fucking Christ, they're only kids."

"I know." I leaned forward, catching his arm and pulling him close so I could speak in his ear. "Don't get mad. They need calm right now."

He nodded, slipping past me, and kneeling in front of the child leading the group. I moved on to the next cage, pulling open the door until I was able to make out the people inside. This one didn't have any more space than the last and was just as packed. Somehow, they had managed to open enough space in the middle of the room so that there was a human-shaped void. The omegas started to flood from the cell to leave me with the image of a woman lying on the floor. There was a man kneeling by her head, he was holding her hand and talking to her in low, hushed tones. Every inch of her skin I could see was covered in bruises. She was barely breathing, which made me nervous. It wasn't until my eyes moved down to the blood that had soaked through the gown she was wearing and pooling on the concrete beneath her that panic seized in my chest.

"BRADLEY!" My scream made all of them jump. I didn't care, she needed my alpha, and she needed him now.

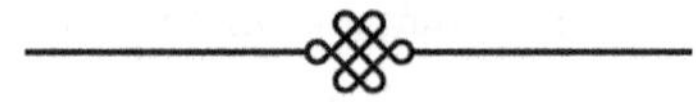

Bradley

I could hear Dante's panicked scream from the front of the house;. I was moving before he finished my name, clearing the door and heading down the basement stairs as quickly as I could. Dante was standing in front of one of the cells, his eyes filled with relief when he saw me. I was at his side before he could say anything. "Tell me what happened."

"Why do you care?" The voice made my head turn to see a man kneeling next to a woman who was in a bad way.

My pulse quickened as I took in the woman on the floor. She was losing entirely too much blood, and I couldn't tell where it was coming from, especially from this distance. I worked up a list of things I would need in my mind as I responded to the omega kneeling by her head. "It's my job to care."

"At least you're honest."

"May I?" I held my hands out so he could see they were empty. When he nodded, I moved forward until I could kneel at her feet. I tried to categorize the wounds as I held my hand out behind me. Dante put my medical bag in my hand, which I took and sat beside me. Opening it up, I grabbed my trauma shears and sliced through her gown in one quick motion. She was covered in bruises and was bleeding from at least five places from what I could see. The wounds were fresh, still raised and open, that concerned me more than anything. I flinched when I saw where all the blood was coming from as her thighs were covered in it. Reaching into my bag again I turned to the omega. "I'm going to need your help...."

"Marshall."

I nodded to him. "Marshall." I grabbed the bag of saline from my bag and handed it to him. "I need to get fluids into her, pronto." The needle was already in my hand as I shifted to get next to her arm. My fingers found where the largest vein in her arm should have been. I could feel her heartbeat, it was weakening by the second. And worse yet, I couldn't find the damn vein to make the stick. My head turned as I called out to my omega. "Dante, I need the bone drill."

"Why do you need to drill into her bones?" Marcus seemed puzzled at my actions; I was certain he suspected I was just torturing her.

"She's lost too much blood. Her veins have collapsed, I need to get fluids into her, and I need to do it now. The fastest way to do that is to get a needle straight into the bone marrow."

"You can't put it somewhere else?"

I looked up at him from where I knelt. "Not really. Once they have collapsed, the only thing I can do is go for the bone marrow." Dante returned then, setting the drill in my hand, and turning around. I could make out his voice as he calmed the omegas and worked on getting the evacuation groups together. Tuning his voice out, I reached into the kit and grabbed the large gage drill needle to attach to the end of it. My eyes moved up to Marshall. "This isn't going to be pretty."

I didn't wait for him to respond, turning the drill on and aiming for the woman's femur. Pulling the trigger, the needle cut through the skin and muscle until it kicked back as it hit the bone. Putting my weight into the end of it, I could feel the needle fighting the bone as it bore through, it took mere moments to set the needle. Pressing the button to release the needle from the drill, I caught the line in my hand as I set the device on the ground next to me. My hand came up for Marshall to set the saline in my hand. I hooked the line into the bottom of the bag and handed it back to the omega.

"Squeeze, keep it even." He did as I asked, allowing me to move up so I could check on her. Her breaths were barely there, her body was starting to shut down, and all I could do was hope I could keep her alive long enough to do something. I pulled my stethoscope from around my shoulders and placed it to her chest. The beating of her heart was weak, slowing down. "Come on." It skipped for a moment, making me hold my breath. "Come on." There was a moment where the beat disappeared before it surged back, until it was steady. "We need to get her transported, now."

Dante appeared at the opening of the cell, his eyes moving along the woman on the floor. "Is she going to live?"

"For now, I need to get her somewhere I can keep an eye on her." He nodded.

Chapter 43

Dante

We had spent the rest of the night getting everyone settled into the temporary rooms Amani had created in her shelter. Over the next few weeks she would work through them and figure out their needs and wants. When she announced that anyone who wanted to leave was welcome to, I had nearly interrupted her until she reminded me what she did only helped if they wanted help. No one left, all of them seemed to be in shock.

"It's okay," Amani whispered in my ear. "Some will filter off over time, others will want to stay. We did what we could."

She led my pack into her inner sanctum, the stairs opening up to what would have been a large living room if my pack hadn't been filling it. Penelope was sitting in Rhys's lap, pulling out of his arms to come to me. I pulled her into my arms, burying my face in her neck, I felt like I was home. Taking a deep breath, I sighed in relief; it wasn't until I took a second breath that it hit me. There was a slight tang to her scent now, adding to it in a mouthwatering way; it made my cock throb. I couldn't want her any more than I did right at that moment. I didn't want to release her, and I had an overwhelming urge to carry her to the bed and serve her every whim.

"I have something I need to tell you," she whispered into my chest.

I stepped back enough to be able to see her beautiful face. "You're pregnant."

"How did you know?"

"An omega always knows." We shared a laugh at our old inside joke.

The ground shook around us as alarms started to blare. My head turned in time to catch Amani moving to the wall. She pulled a panel open, typing a code into it caused slams to echo above us. Putting in another code, she pulled up a live feed that showed the warehouse surrounded by black SUVs. Reaching over, she silenced the alarms as she grabbed a phone that hung beside the panel. Bringing it to her ear, she spoke into the receiver, her words coming through the speakers mounted in the corner of the rooms. "We are under attack, proceed to the designated evacuation tunnels. I repeat, we are under attack, proceed to the designated evacuation tunnels."

"Did we check everyone for trackers?" I hoped Richie had.

"There were too many," Richie explained, "there wasn't time."

"Fuck," I growled.

"It doesn't matter." Amani was already moving, crossing the room to open a panel that was filled with guns. "This ends now."

Penelope moved to arm herself, but I stopped her by grabbing her arm. "You're pregnant, absolutely not. You evacuate."

"You are, too." Dorian spoke then, coming up beside Amani. "You need to take Daniella and go."

"I'm not giving up my home without a fight," she insisted.

"They're both right," Xavier spoke then. "You need to go with Penelope, little sister."

"No," Amani hissed, "I know my property better than anyone else."

She had a point. "Can you direct us from here?"

"I can."

I nodded. "Why don't you do that while Penelope and your omega evacuate with Daniella?"

No one liked that idea, they all looked at me as if I had all the answers. Urban warfare was my specialty behind blacksmithing; my hand ached for a mallet right now. I planned the building out in my head, trying to place everyone based on their strengths. Once again, Rhys and Ares were the unknowns, making them my secret weapons. They wouldn't see me coming, either, with my specialized training. Bradley was more of a backup person, but he was a fighter through and through. He was a second wave person. We could send him and Dorian in to scatter the attackers, sending them right into the traps Richie would lay. Xavier was our last line of defense. He wouldn't like it one bit, but his training was specialized to the point he was highly effective one on one, but not as skilled against groups.

"Rhys, go." My voice was closer to a bark than it had ever been. Xavier came to me, pulling me into his arms and pressing his forehead to mine. "Take Ares with you." I looked up at my alpha, he was always the strongest of us. My eyes turned to Richie. "Go make your traps." Xavier started to pull away from me but I stopped him. "Stay with me."

"I'm not going anywhere." His response was enough to make me release him.

I turned in time to catch Bradley pressing a kiss to Penelope's lips. He came to me, sweeping me into his arms. I was lost as he spun me around, his lips catching mine. When he set me on my feet, I smiled at him. "Be careful."

I watched as he and Dorian disappeared up the stairs, I couldn't help but feel like I was sending them to their deaths. Running across the space, I watched the cameras over Amani's shoulder. There was something wrong, and I couldn't quite place what it was. I caught Rhys first, his was really an elegant dance of death, his blades working themselves through his opponents. He was there one moment and then gone the next, seeming to teleport around the area. My eyes moved to the next camera, it was Richie, leading a group of SWAT officers down a hall. When they crossed into the communal dining room, the last of them tripped on a wire, sending the rest of them to the ground.

I started to search for Bradley when I felt the first coil of panic start to wrap around my heart. Penelope came up behind me, her hand on my shoulder. "I can feel it too."

Something was very wrong. Struggling to control my breathing, I searched the cameras for my alphas. The screens were going black one by one. Searching the bonds, I could tell they were alive, but I had no idea what was happening. "Time to go." Xavier's voice made me turn to him. The pain slammed into me as Xavier caught my hand, he was dragging me and Penelope toward the back of the room.

To be continued...

Acknowledgements

Thank you to my mother for editing this for me and putting up with every breakdown when I lost this over and over. Thanks to Nicole at Naughty Nook PR for the blurb, proofreading, and formatting. A special thank you to Lo at Hey Book Bestie Author Services for sensitivity reading this for me. I wish I still had the post that inspired this, but thank you to whoever asked for the pack to focus on the new omega instead of their established one, this book really would not exist without you.

www.ingramcontent.com/pod-product-compliance
Lightning Source LLC
LaVergne TN
LVHW010650110826
845149LV00014B/3023